REPUTATIO

Lucinda: She wanted passionately to live up to Derek's ideals, and after all, the past was dead. Derek was her future. But she was still afraid.

Derek: He of all people must never know about her past. He would be bitterly disillusioned. Or would he love her enough to believe in her? Would he?

Max: Powerful, fiercely protective. He had to warn his brother and save him from this marriage.

Also by the same author

The Noble One
The Strange Meeting
Climb To The Stars
The Untrodden Snow
Gypsy Lover
House of The Seventh Cross
Wait For Tomorrow
I Should Have Known
Love And Desire And Hate
The Unlit Fire
Brief Ecstasy
You Have Chosen
Shatter The Sky
Those Who Love
Swing of Youth
Arrow In The Heart
All That Matters
A Love Like Ours
Put Back The Clock
Strange Rapture
The Wild Bird

and available in Coronet Books

Reputation

Denise Robins

CORONET BOOKS
Hodder Paperbacks Ltd., London

Copyright © 1963 by Denise Robins
First Published January 1963
by Hodder & Stoughton Ltd
Coronet Edition 1965
Second Impression 1972

Printed in Great Britain
for Coronet Books, Hodder Paperbacks Ltd.,
St Paul's House, Warwick Lane, London, E.C.4,
by Richard Clay (The Chaucer Press), Ltd.,
Bungay, Suffolk

ISBN 0 340 16081 0

For
my good doctor,
JAMES BARRIE
and for
MARGARET
and
THE BOYS

I

LUCINDA was five minutes late for work that morning.

It was a wet, windy morning in August, not at all the right sort of weather for the summer. All the girls who worked at Ruchelle's had scurried into the shop this morning wearing macintosh coats and hoods and carrying umbrellas which would scarcely stay up because of the wind. They all grumbled as they gathered in the little room that they used at the back of the big salon which faced Knightsbridge. Somebody switched on an electric fire. The girls dried wet, silken ankles. But when Lucinda Mace joined the group, she looked as though it was a bright spring day. She, too, was soaked but her face was radiant. There was a sparkle in her large eyes which none of the others had seen before.

"I say, Cindy," said one of them as she pinned up three damp curls in front of the mirror, "where were *you* last night? Out with a millionaire? Or have you won a football pool?"

Lucinda laughed back. That, too, was something she didn't do very often. She was usually such a quiet, reserved sort of girl. When the others chatted during tea-break or after hours about their conquests, their ambitions, their parties, Cindy kept quiet. It had always been an astonishment to them that she rarely seemed to go out on parties or have a boy friend. Of course everybody knew that she had had bad luck at home. Her father used to be quite well-off but had lost his money, and her mother's health wasn't very good. They knew and respected the fact that Cindy took her pay-packet home instead of spending it on herself, and nobody was jealous of her. She had no enemies. She was generous and friendly and they liked her despite her reticence. She was always doing a good turn to somebody. Even Madame Colette, who was the manageress and a bit of an old tartar, had a soft spot for Lucinda. Nobody could deny that Cindy worked hard and put through as many, if not more, sales than most of them.

"Something's happened to you, Cindy. You might let us in on it," said the first girl who had spoken.

Madame Colette's voice rose sharply, from the salon.

"*Mes enfants*, come along! We will have customers in a moment. Stop chattering, please."

But the girls crowded around Lucinda. Amongst other things this morning they had never seen her look so attractive. She had woken up. She *glowed* and it suited her. Everybody thought she was far too modest. She was so attractive. A little on the thin side, perhaps, but her figure was beautiful and she had that rich red-brown hair which reminded one of horse-chestnuts in the sun. Her heavily lashed eyes were as greeny-blue as the sea, and she had a slightly retroussé nose thickly dusted with golden freckles. Monsieur Ruchelle, the proprietor who came regularly over from Paris with 'models', always called her 'The Honeypot'. He tried to flirt with her. But he didn't get far. No man found it easy to get on intimate terms with Lucinda.

Now, quickly, she held out the left hand which she had been shyly holding behind her back. The girls saw the small ruby and diamond ring on the slender finger. A little squeal of delight went up.

"*Cindy!* You're *engaged!*"

"Yes," she breathed.

"Tell us . . . tell us about it."

"*Mes enfants!*" interrupted the impatient voice of Madame, "a customer. Lucinda . . . Bettina . . . quickly, please."

The news that they were agog to hear had to wait until lunch-time. Then she told them.

His name was Derek Chalmerson. She had met him at the house of her great friend Iris Turnbull, who lived at Putney where the Maces also had a house. Iris worked as a secretary in a firm of manufacturing chemists. Derek was a bio-chemist there.

"Any money?" asked Madame Colette, who was also listening to the news from her favourite vendeuse. Madame was a true Frenchwoman. She had a great regard for money.

Cindy sparkled at her.

"Not much money but he's absolutely sweet. I adore him."

They pressed her for further details. Laughingly, Cindy warded them off but admitted that it was not a sudden affair. She and Derek had known each other now for several months. She had been out with him but hadn't said much to anybody. It was her nature to be cautious, she said, and she had wanted to be quite sure about Derek. Last night he had given her this ring. On Saturday week there was to be a party at the Savoy to celebrate the engagement, and her twenty-first birthday, at the same time.

She was kissed and congratulated. Appropriately, the sun came out as she left the shop. And it was a real August sun. It beat down warmly from a fast clearing sky.

Derek was there to meet her.

One or two girls watched from behind the glass door of the shop and looked with approval at the young man as he took her arm and walked away with her. Definitely a good-looker was the verdict; fair with blue eyes and the strong, clean look of a typical English boy. He could not be all that much older than Lucinda, they thought. He wore nicely cut grey flannels, and he certainly looked as though he was in love. Lucky Cindy! She had found her man. No girl alive but would envy another girl *that* good fortune.

As they walked down toward the Brompton Road, Lucinda looked up at her newly made fiancé. He was fingering the little ruby ring on her finger and regarding it, then said with pride:

"So you're still wearing it."

"Idiot," she laughed. "I haven't had it off all night. I was so thrilled. Mummy and Daddy are thrilled, too. They like you so much, Derek."

"It's decent of them," he said. "I only wish I had more to offer you."

"But you're going a long way—everybody says how brilliant you are."

"You flatter me, darling," he said. "I can hardly believe you've said 'yes'. I'm damned lucky."

"No, I am," she said seriously.

"No," he disagreed, "you deserve something *much* more . . ."

For a single instant the glow vanished from Lucinda's eyes. An echo of the past that she had been trying for a long time to wipe from her memory stirred, and troubled her again.

I don't deserve Derek. I don't deserve anything as good or fine, the thought leapt to her mind.

It was strange that lunch with Derek, in one of their favourite restaurants, was not as happy for Lucinda as it should have been. But Derek positively beamed. He spent money in a lordly way and insisted on opening a bottle of wine to share with her. He held her hand under the table. He kept telling her that she was the most beautiful thing on God's earth and that she looked 'heavenly' in her rose-pink linen suit, and that he regretted that *he* had neither mother nor father to welcome her into the Chalmerson family. His only living relative was a brother and Max was miles away in Kenya where he had been working for the last few years.

"I shall send an air-letter to Max today," Derek announced. "I'll tell him all about you. And you must give me a photograph to send him, so that he can see how beautiful you are. But the one thing I'll never be able to tell him is how terrifically *good* you are as well as lovely. There's something quite angelic about you, my Lucinda."

She remained silent. She felt a distinct sense of unease. A distaste for these repeated compliments because she felt them to be undeserved. She said, quite sharply:

"I'm not all that angelic. I'm . . . just ordinary. Please don't idealise me."

"Leave me to be the judge of that," said Derek grandly, then added: "Tell me again that you love me. I can't believe that you really do."

Now she answered with all the warmth and tenderness in her nature.

"I do love you, Derek darling, and I'm going to be the happiest girl in the world when I marry you."

"We get on so well together," he said, with a deep, fond look at her.

She had been unhappy for so long that it seemed difficult for her to believe that she had found this great, absorbing love. Derek was so 'special'.

Yet when they first met she had not been particularly impressed. In her teens she used to like a man to be smooth and posed and glamorous, rather of the film-star variety. Derek had no such appeal. His thick fair hair, in school-boy manner, refused to lie down. His eyes were brightly blue under thick fair brows. He was a little shy. His hobbies were stamp-collecting (he was a first-class philatelist); and he had a passion for veteran cars. He actually owned a wonderful old 1920 Bugatti. He spent a lot of his spare time polishing the brasses and 'topping-up' the engine. The car was known as *Mr. Moses*. *Mr. Moses* amused Lucinda and always brought the dimples to her cheeks. She enjoyed going out in the old car with Derek. They entered the London-to-Brighton rally together, which thrilled her even though they didn't do well. Derek said she looked ravishing in her old motoring cap with a chiffon veil tied under her chin. It was then he had first fallen in love with her, he said.

She, herself, had suddenly opened up, like a flower that has been too long denied the sun, under the warmth of Derek's whole-hearted admiration. He told her that she was the first girl he had even taken seriously. He was only three years older than herself. Years ago she might have found him too smug and unimaginative. But last night when she melted into his arms and felt his clean, boyish lips on hers, she also felt the moment to be quite sacramental. The beginning of something real and wonderful in her life. He offered all the security and integrity she seemed so far to have lacked.

"I can't think why you love me," she had said humbly, as they sat in *Mr. Moses* in a quiet, secluded road on Putney Heath. Derek pressed his warm cheek against hers.

"Because you aren't like other girls, always careering around with boy friends. You *look* terrific, but you aren't one of those sex-kittens, I can't stand that type. But you—oh, gosh! I felt half afraid to ask you to kiss me, until tonight."

"Don't make an idol of me, please . . ."

"You *are* in a way my idol, and I want to adore you," he added with touching fervour.

She was immensely touched, yet she was still afraid.

The past was over but pasts have an ugly way of creeping back into the present. Hadn't somebody once said that '*old sins have long shadows*'? It wasn't that she had *sinned* but everybody else *thought* she had. Derek would only have to meet somebody who *knew* about that affair and he would be bitterly disillusioned.

Now they sat in the restaurant smoking their cigarettes and drinking coffee. Derek made plans for their future. He expected to get a new and better job in the large factory which his firm were building near Horsham, in Sussex. They must get married soon and buy a cottage.

"Let's have a short engagement," he said. And he talked of an early wedding. They'd drive away from the church in *Mr. Moses*—he grinned happily. Lucinda's spirits soared. She must draw a veil over the past and blot it right out from her memory, she decided.

"Oh, darling *Mr. Moses*!" she sighed, and was happy again.

She telephoned the news to her godmother, Lady Hordham, that night. Lady Hordham was a wealthy widow living in a block of flats in Lowndes Square. She had been at school with Lucinda's mother.

"I thought that Derek a very nice boy when you brought

him to see me the other day," she said. "I'm sure your parents will be just as pleased as I am. From what they tell me, Derek is a very clever young man."

"But I'm a little worried, Aunt Mary," said Lucinda.

"What about, child?"

"He's so full of ideals. Frightfully high-minded. Don't you think I ought to tell him about . . . about . . ."

Lady Hordham interrupted sharply.

"Don't be so absurd! Under no circumstances. *That* was your past. Derek is your future. You are not to say one word."

"Very well," said Lucinda meekly.

Derek was warmly received by Lucinda's parents and friends. Not for two long years had she been so happy.

But she did hope Aunt Mary had given her the right advice. The more she saw of Derek the more convinced she became that he would be horrified if he ever learned about the thing that had happened when she was eighteen.

Toward the end of the following week, Derek had some exciting news to give her.

Max, his half-brother, to whom he was devoted, was flying home. He was going to be at the engagement party.

"It's a terrific thrill for me," Derek told her. "The one person whom I value in the world, next to you, is Max. He's such a marvellous person. He's six years older than I am. We had the same father. After my mother's death he took care of me. He has always done everything. I went out to Nairobi twelve months ago for my holiday. He even paid my fare—so I could be with him. He isn't married. I can't think why not," Derek added with a laugh. "He's considered jolly attractive by the girls. But if he has one fault it is that he is a bit of a cynic. He's so good-looking, girls fall over themselves about him and I think he distrusts them. He hasn't been as lucky as I am, you see. There aren't many lovely girls as worthwhile as my Lucinda."

"I wish you wouldn't keep saying these things," she exclaimed sharply.

Derek stared at her.

"What's wrong with you?" he asked in a puzzled voice.

She bit her lip and looked down at her ring.

"Nothing," she said. "I'm just . . . silly."

Ten days later she and her parents drove to the Savoy to attend the party Aunt Mary was giving for her. And on this occasion she felt no qualms—nothing but happiness and excitement.

Lady Hordham, her godmother, was a generous hostess and Cindy was pleased that her friend Iris was present with a delightful boy friend. Iris, who had stood by her so loyally through the dark days of two summers ago.

When Derek saw his fiancée he told her that he was 'dazzled'.

She was certainly glamorous tonight in white pleated chiffon—a graceful, simply cut evening dress which made her look very appealing. Her red-brown hair was parted in the centre and brushed up in thick waves over her ears. She wore no jewellery except Derek's ring and the ruby earrings her parents had given her for an engagement present.

"Has Max come?" she asked Derek. When she had telephoned him earlier in the day the half-brother had still not arrived. Derek had booked a room in a hotel near him. Derek, himself, shared a flat with another young bio-chemist from his factory and had no room for Max. Besides, as Derek had laughingly told Lucinda, Max was the rich one. He had a very good Government job in Kenya and had done well, and wanted a good hotel for his holiday.

"He's a grand person. I'm longing for him to meet you," Derek said. "You'll be most impressed, I'm sure. And it's just 'made' my night having him with us."

Lucinda was equally anxious to see Max. She had heard so much about him. Derek hero-worshipped him. Max's word, Max's ideas, Max's wishes, were law with Derek.

"I know Max! We needn't worry," Derek told Lucinda. "If he says he's going to do a thing, he'll do it. If he has to drop down on the Embankment in a *helicopter* he'll arrive in one. You'll see!"

The little party had scarcely sat down and ordered their aperitifs before Derek sprang up again, his blue eyes shining.

"He's here. Look, Lucinda—that's Max."

Eagerly she followed his gaze. She had to admit that the tall young man striding across the room toward them was most extraordinarily good-looking.

Taller than Derek, Max Chalmerson stood at least six-foot-four—wide-shouldered, slim-hipped, with the lean, vital look of a man who has spent a lot of time out-of-doors. He made every other man in this room look pallid. He gave the impression of great physical strength. He gave her only a cursory glance then turned to his half-brother.

"Derek! So I've made it. Sorry to be late, old boy. My plane was delayed, and I had to change."

"This is great!" exclaimed Derek. "Let me introduce you to my fiancée, Lucinda Mace. Lucinda . . . Max."

Lucinda held out her hand. But the smile that Max Chalmerson had given his young brother—swift, warm, friendly—vanished as he turned to her. His eyes—they were light grey and had a curiously magnetic quality—held hers with a hard, critical sort of glance that confounded her. It was not at all the sort of look she had expected. There was nothing warm or welcoming in his voice as he said:

"How d'you do . . ."

He doesn't like me, she thought, dismayed. *I can't understand it. Why doesn't he?*

Then Max said:

"Incidentally, this is a small world. I'd no sooner put foot into the Savoy before I ran into a friend. She was in Nairobi all this last year and a great friend of mine. She came back to London two days before me. There she is—that woman in red . . . just dancing past us now."

Derek took little interest in Max's friend. He was saying eagerly:

"Let me introduce you to my future in-laws, Max."

But Lucinda stood like a frozen image. All her colour had gone and her eyes were full of horror.

She knew that woman in red. She knew her very well. Her name was Vivian Brill-Burrie. She was staring over her partner's shoulders at Lucinda as she danced by, and smiling, a cold deadly little smile. The one thing that Lucinda had feared . . . that dark, dangerous shadow of the unforgotten past had risen to confront her now in earnest, black and menacing. The worst ghost of all, she thought—Vivian, who had been her most bitter and treacherous enemy. And by the worst bits of bad luck, she knew Max—and at any moment Cindy was sure Max would want to introduce Vivian to Derek.

So, Lucinda thought, the axe has fallen, and on the very night of my engagement party. I might have known I wouldn't be allowed to stay happy. *I might have known.*

Derek caught her hand. He was pressing it in his warm fingers. The others were toasting them with raised goblets of champagne. Max, too, raised his glass and looked straight into Lucinda's eyes. But the very expression in them devastated her.

He knows, she thought. Vivian must have told him out there in Nairobi when Derek's letter about his engagement had first arrived.

The waiters were handing them menus.

"Let's choose what we want to eat, darling," said Derek, putting an arm around her and looking over her shoulder at the menu he put into her cold fingers.

The band was playing a twist. People were dancing. It was a gay, glittering world. But to Lucinda it might not have existed. She felt strangely isolated—almost as though she had no right to be here at all. Her thoughts were sliding away on a desperate torrent. The past lived again.

Lucinda was eighteen years old.

2

IT had all happened that summer at the Alexandra Hotel, Oversands-by-Sea.

Lucinda was one of a party. All of them were in the same crowd in Putney. This was a huge modern hotel with glass windows and luxury rooms. Oversands nestled in a sheltered bay, and it had a tiny quay, and many people came here for the sailing. There was a good beach and a delightful background of green undulating countryside. Sixty miles out of London, it was still unspoilt.

Vivian Brill-Burrie had actually been the one to organise the holiday. Her husband, a busy osteopath, had managed to bring her down. Then there was Tommy Marchent, an Oxford undergraduate, one of young Cindy's many admirers; and a pretty, but rather empty-headed girl named Zoë Ennerman with her rich, doting husband. And, of course, Lucinda's godmother, Lady Hordham.

It had been fine to begin with but on that one day that stuck so firmly and bitterly in Lucinda's memory, it was raining.

Lucinda in those days was a great tennis enthusiast. She had hoped for a game with Tommy this afternoon. But it wasn't possible. Tommy, a pleasant if rather empty-headed young man, announced that he was going upstairs to change and that Lucinda had better do the same. On a day like this it would be table-tennis if anything, he said ruefully.

"Oh, what a bind!" exclaimed Cindy.

Two small boys in jeans and T-shirts rushed up to her.

"Cindy, Cindy, come and play Indians with us."

The girl put an arm around both and grinned at Tommy.

"That's an idea. You might be the Big White Chief, Tom."

"What—and you as a squaw?" he grinned back. "Can't say you've ever struck me as the type to make a squaw."

"How wrong you are. I'm just a little squaw at heart, longing to follow my Man wherever he goes. Me Laughing Water, makee good grub for Hiawatha!"

She thumped her chest and emitted a loud war-cry. The small boys joined in. Two elderly women sitting in the lounge looked up from their knitting. One of them whispered to the other:

"It really is shocking the way that girl behaves. Anybody would think she was the same age as those boys."

"It's about all she is," said the other woman, cattily.

An elderly curate who sat with them gave a smile.

"I don't think either of you have got it quite right," he said mildly. "Little Miss Mace has a heart of gold. When she isn't playing tennis, which one must say is an innocuous pastime, she's being kind and thoughtful to others. She keeps the children amused and once when I asked her to go and read to that poor half-blind Mrs. Simpkins, she did so without hesitation. I find her a very much higher type than some of these so-called young Beatnik ladies of the day."

After which the curate departed. One of the women put her tongue in her cheek. She was watching Lucinda solemnly marching behind Tommy with the two boys behind her, all of them talking gibberish which was meant to be the Indian tongue and brandishing tennis racquets as imaginary hatchets.

"That childish play can cover up a lot that the dear curate doesn't see," she said. "For instance, there's the business of *the doctor*."

"You mean Dr. Brill-Burrie . . ."

"Yes. They say he wasn't so keen on doctoring so turned to osteopathy. He had quite a good practice in Putney. His wife is sweet. Suffers terribly from migraine. Older than he is, and I don't think he treats her too well."

"Oh, I've heard that, too! And whenever she's laid up, I notice Lucinda Mace goes after him."

"*After* him?" repeated the other woman with delight in this gossip, since she had nothing better to do than to listen to the rumours. "Well I never! Do you suppose he is interested in *her*?"

"Oh, I doubt that," but here, the chief gossip of the hotel stopped and returned to her knitting with a warning silence. "Ssh, here he comes."

Dr. Wilfred Brill-Burrie walked through the lounge. He paused to light a cigarette and saw the pretty, eighteen-year-old girl who was zig-zagging around the lounge with the children. She was like a child herself, he thought. In his opinion she had plenty of what the French call 'allure'. Yet she was a woman. One who seemed unconscious of the power she had to attract the opposite sex.

He liked her—but feared for her. He felt a tired, sad man— old for his thirty years even to the touch of premature grey in his hair. He was at the moment bitterly conscious of the fact that he could not get close to the wife whom ten years ago he had married with such love. He had thought Vivian loved him, too. Perhaps she had done so at the beginning but there had been no children and they had drifted apart. She perpetually whined and complained about her health although her medical advisors assured him there was nothing really wrong with her and that it was all in her mind. She was thoroughly discontented. But she was still beautiful. Everybody admired her. Yet she didn't seem to keep her friends. Wilfred had noticed that.

He was no longer sure of her—or of himself. He had begun to feel he had made a poor choice, yet he was trying desperately to keep the ship afloat. At the moment he wondered if a certain man down here was not trying to get Vivian away from him. She had certainly made it plain since they arrived that she wanted to get away from *him*. She really wanted a *divorce*. She had actually said so but he told her he refused to contemplate the idea.

Now the sight of pretty, gay Lucinda made him remember

how last night when he and Vivian were having one of their frequent disputes she had brought up Cindy's name.

"A cheap coquette," Vivian had called her.

He didn't really believe that. He was sure that Lucinda Mace was not deliberately provocative. She was only eighteen, still a débutante. And always rather nice and kind to him. Tried to include him in her little parties when Vivian was having one of her 'turns'.

Young Cindy had a zest for life which Dr. Brill-Burrie envied. He couldn't understand the way Vivian spoke behind the girl's back. She always seemed on the best of terms with her in public. He had heard her telling Cindy how pretty she was, and what a lovely skin she had, and so on. Then up in her room, she would say:

"Don't forget that chit is only eighteen and she *ought* to have a good skin, and no lines. *I'm* nearly thirty-three. I shall soon be forty and old. I *hate* girls like Lucinda. They make me *feel* a hundred."

Then she would begin to cry.

No, he couldn't understand Vivian any more.

"You're becoming neurotic," he told her last night. She had spun round at him, her eyes flashing. She had long amber-coloured, magnificent eyes, rather like a cat's. She made the sort of malicious remark that puzzled him.

"I know you think it's all nerves with me, but *I* know some-body else who thinks I deserve a better fate than having to live in Putney as your wife. I need to be petted and spoiled and to live in the South of France."

But when Wilfred asked her who said this, she had merely tossed her head and lapsed into sullen silence. They hadn't been getting on for so long now that he had almost retired from the efforts to please her and flung himself body and soul into his practice in Putney.

The children had gone—reluctantly answering a call from their mother.

Tommy Marchent had departed, singing:

"Cindy, oh Cindy,
Cindy don't let me down,
Write me a letter soon,
And I'll be homeward bound."

Cindy, racquet under arm, saw Wilfred and came up to him with her friendly, brilliant smile.

"Hello, there, doc. I'm frozen in these shorts. Think Tommy's right. One might as well give up."

"It's been a rotten summer so far," he sighed. "I don't know why we all stay down here. Better off back in Town."

"Oh, but it is still a lot of fun," exclaimed Lucinda. "I'm adoring it. Look at that stormy sea. It's rather splendid."

"You adore *life*, don't you?" he smiled.

"Oh, yes," she breathed ecstatically.

At that moment an extremely handsome young man wearing a blazer stalked through the lounge. He grinned at Cindy and nodded. She nodded back, then, cheeks burning, turned to Wilfred, and pressed her hands dramatically to her breast.

"Oo, isn't he *gorgeous!*"

"He's just a film star," said Wilfred a trifle stiffly.

"He 'sends' me," murmured Lucinda.

"I really don't know what that means."

Stuffy old thing, she thought, yet she was always sorry for him. He seemed a nice, gentle sort of man. But Lucinda liked his wife, too. She had been really rather flattering and helped Cindy with clothes and make-up and all the things she understood. She was nearly fourteen years older than Lucinda, herself; she had travelled a lot and played the piano well—light stuff. One night there'd been a party here and Vivian had been a huge success. She wore stunning clothes that suited her dark, piled-up hair, amber eyes and olive skin. Cindy thought her wonderful and envied Vivian her poise and sophistication. Besides, it was so sad she should be so delicate. But Cindy usually tried to be nice to Wilfred—just because he was dull and seemed to lag so far behind his wife.

Once, when Lucinda was a little girl her mother had said to her:

"We *can't* keep all the stray dogs and cats you bring home, Cindy. You've got far too big a heart. You must learn to control it."

But no, she never had really been able to control that longing to be especially nice to those who seemed in need of 'niceness'. She had been constantly in trouble at school, and later at college, because of her mischievous escapades. She adored 'fun'.

"What are you going to do, doc?" she asked Wilfred. "Are you taking Vivian out?"

"No—she's lying down."

"Well, I'm booked to play table-tennis with the twins. I was playing Indians with them just now."

"I saw you."

"*You* could play with us," suggested Lucinda, giggling. But she didn't in the least want him to accept the invitation.

"I'm going for a walk," he replied, hastily.

"Do you know," she added confidingly, "our film star has just let it be known that he's got a wife in Hollywood, which is a jolly shame because I've got a terrific 'thing' about him. We went swimming together yesterday and I got cramp and he had to pull me in. It was *terrific*."

Dr. Brill-Burrie had an uneasy recollection of all the things his wife kept saying about this girl. He decided suddenly to give the silly child a friendly warning.

"You just simmer down, dear. People talk, you know."

The smile vanished from Lucinda's charming face. She looked suddenly uncomfortable.

"I don't know what you mean."

"I mean sometimes you are apt to be too free-and-easy with your 'gorgeous film stars' and . . . and so on . . ." he stopped, feeling slightly foolish. There was such complete innocence in the clear eyes Lindy raised to him. She laughed.

"I see! You've been listening to the gossip about me. Oh

yes, Tommy tells me there's plenty and that I'm supposed to be Play-Girl number one of the party. But I think people are horrible. They always think the worst and the 'worser' they think, the more it makes me want to play the fool and shock them."

He coughed.

"Just watch your step or you might . . ."

"I might get my wings singed. Cindy, the poor little moth . . .!"

Her laughter rippled out again. Lucinda was nothing if not defiant. She could never resist a challenge. She knew she was doing nothing wrong. If all the old cats in the hotel liked to come to wrong conclusions, *let* them.

She walked away from Wilfred and took the lift up to the third floor to her bedroom. It was disgracefully untidy. She made some effort to put things away as she changed out of her shorts into slacks and a bright pink pullover.

They had a dance here every night so Mummy had bought her two dinner dresses. One of them hung outside the wardrobe. Blue taffeta. She wished it was a bit more *chic* like the gorgeous dresses Vivian Brill-Burrie wore. She must ask Viv what jewellery she ought to wear with this blue dress; her two rows of pearls or her blue beads to match the dress. She had such a *respect* for Vivian's taste. She wasn't like that awful Zoë Ennerman. Zoë was only about five years older than Cindy but already married and to a wealthy 'tycoon' who came down at week-ends to join her. He showered her with presents. Tommy had nicknamed her 'Twinkle' because she wore so much jewellery. She positively glittered with diamonds at night. Everybody thought it such bad taste.

Lucinda felt a little put out by Dr. Brill-Burrie's suggestion that she should 'simmer down' because people were talking about her. That life-saving incident. It was so unfair. It hadn't meant a *thing*, for instance, either to the film star or to her. She wasn't *really* in love with him, nor he, at all, with her. She was just in love with life and glamour and she had had any number of 'pin-ups' since she was sixteen. Old Wilf, as she and Tommy called the doctor, was just like Mummy and Daddy. They didn't really understand teenagers or how much better it is to shut one's mind to all the terrible things that can happen, and enjoy one's life.

Lucinda had her solemn moments. But she didn't intend to settle down just *yet*.

"You must get down to some serious work and do a little less of this rushing round with all the boys, living in the tennis club or going out to all those parties," Mummy had said just before Lucinda left home. "Your father and I know how absolutely innocent you are, darling, but it's a cruel, harsh world—a girl has *got* to mind her p's and q's when she's as pretty as you are."

Then she had reminded Cindy of the milk-lorry affair.

That was always being pushed at her, thought Cindy, who could still giggle about it even now, though it happened a year ago. It was after her seventeenth birthday party. The doors of their nice home in Putney had been opened wide to most of the young people in the neighbourhood. When the party was over, somebody had dared Cindy to drive round London on a milk-lorry and help deliver milk, wearing full evening dress. She had done it. But just because the lorry-driver was a young, good-looking boy, the older people had raised their brows and suggested something worse.

Cindy kept saying to her mother:

"My motto is 'Evil be to him who evil thinks'."

This usually brought another rebuke from Mummy.

"You've got to accept the world as it is and one day you'll get into serious trouble if you aren't careful."

Lucinda, in the midst of tidying her room, heard a tap on the door. She was delighted to see Vivian, herself, standing there.

"Oh, hello, do come in, Vivian. I thought your husband said you were not very well."

"Thanks—I'm better now," murmured Vivian Brill-Burrie, and sauntered into the room. Unlike Cindy, who was tall, she was *petite*—in fact from a distance she might have been the same age as the younger girl. It was only when one got nearer that one noticed the mouth and the petulant lines. A student of human nature might also have mistrusted the way she had of narrowing those amber eyes and looking through her lashes. But she could be very appealing and had a plaintive 'baby' voice and a way of appearing tired and sad. Cindy, so enormously vital and happy, felt sorry for Vivian. Cindy's father, at home, was one of her great admirers, too. In fact, most men 'fell' for Vivian. She moved round the room now, chatting to the younger girl, admiring the blue taffeta dress and advising her to wear the pearls rather than the blue necklace tonight.

"You *are* sweet, and so helpful to me!" exclaimed Lucinda.

Vivian sat down. She twisted her lips. She looked down at her cigarette end. She supposed that Cindy was as stupidly naïve as she appeared, but how she *loathed* all that youth and joyousness when she, herself, was so out of countenance with the world.

Wilfred bored her to death. If only she could get free! But *he* still seemed to want her. She would never get a divorce unless she could 'cook up something' against him. How she envied Lucinda for being so unfettered—and so *healthy*. Vivian really *did* suffer from migraine.

She was quite egotistical and unscrupulous. Nothing mattered to her but her own happiness. She hadn't come down here with this young crowd because she felt herself to be one of them, but because it gave her an opportunity to see a certain man who lived in this district and was at the moment just as anxious as Vivian that she should get her freedom. He was an amusing, wealthy man. She would have gone to him if it wasn't that he had reasons for not wishing to be made a co-respondent. Vivian sometimes wondered despairingly if she could ever get her freedom. But today despair had suddenly been replaced by hope. Lying down after lunch she had cooked up a marvellous plan—at the expense of this silly girl Lucinda Mace, with her wide-eyed innocence and love of mischief.

Quite maliciously, Vivian had encouraged every little 'piece of nonsense' that Cindy had perpetrated since she came down here.

"I've been thinking, Cindy," she murmured.

"About what, Vivian?"

Lucinda sat on the edge of the bed swinging her slim, pretty legs and looking with respectful admiration at the older woman. She was so *beautiful*. That canary-yellow sweater and her well-cut black slacks made her look like a handsome boy rather than a woman who'd been married ten years.

"About that awful girl you and I can't stand, Zoë Ennerman."

"Oh, *Twinkle*, as Tommy calls her," nodded Lucinda. "She's atrociously vulgar. She doesn't even deserve such an amusing nickname. I was absolutely furious with her last night."

"Why? When? I didn't know."

"She happened to be sitting in the lounge with us and so was that rather nice girl, Mrs. Robinson, who is on her honeymoon."

"Tell me about it," said Vivian.

Cindy broke in to her story rather hotly. It was obvious to Vivian that she felt deeply about things and particularly disliked people like Mrs. Robinson being made fun of. And of course it had been obvious to Vivian, also, that Mrs. Robinson and her young husband were not well off. The girl wore cheap clothes, *etcetera*. A person with whom Vivian would not waste her time, but Cindy had often declared that she *liked* Judy Robinson because she was genuine and had 'no side'. It appeared that she had been admiring Zoë Ennerman's magnificent diamond brooch.

"You do have some smashing *joolery*," she had said.

Cindy went on:

"And do you know, Vivian, that horrible Zoë actually

touched the earrings Judy was wearing and mentioned that her emeralds must be worth a fortune, knowing perfectly *well* that they were fakes. Poor Mrs. Robinson coloured up and quite frankly admitted they were false and then Zoë invited her to go up and see *her* emeralds. I thought it was disgusting. Oh, I'd like to get even with her and wipe that smirk off her face."

Vivian considered this. She had, as a matter of fact, just come out of Zoë Ennerman's bedroom. She knew exactly where it was in relation to Cindy's. A very unpleasant idea seized her.

"Well, why not try to get even, dear," she purred in her smooth cat's cream voice.

"How, Vivian?"

"I have a suggestion to make to you."

"Well, if it's a good one I'll say 'yes' to it because I just can't forget Mrs. Robinson's mortified expression and I'll jolly well do anything to upset Zoë. She was too beastly."

"Well, listen to this . . ." said Vivian. "You know her bedroom is three along from yours and they all have connecting balconies. You could climb from your balcony to the next one and so to hers, late tonight when everybody is in bed. You'd get through the windows, touch Zoë, and when she wakes up forbid her to scream and demand in a deep bass voice that she hands over her jewellery."

Lucinda considered this—the light of battle in her eye.

Vivian went on:

"Before she switches on the light and sees you, you can get out and run back to your room. By that time she'll be calling 'blue murder'. We'll all be outside and we'll all rush in."

"Good lord!" exclaimed Cindy, doubtfully.

Vivian wheedled.

"She'll never stop nattering about the cat-burglar who got away. She'll be in a frenzy and put all her diamonds in the hotel safe. The hotel is dead at the moment. This will add a zip to things. It will be enormous fun."

"Well, I must admit it would be just what Zoë deserves. Can I tell Tommy?——" began Lucinda.

Vivian broke in hastily.

"No, don't tell *anybody*. They may try to stop you. It's our secret. It'll be all the more fun when it comes out."

Lucinda pictured herself climbing over the balconies and creeping into Zoë's bedroom. It would certainly teach her a lesson. She would not upset a nice, less pretentious girl like Mrs. Robinson again.

Besides, thought Lucinda with a touch of unusual bitterness, *they all expect me to do something crazy, so I might as well do it. 'Give a dog a bad name and hang him.' How true! Just because I've been involved in one or two escapades!*

Her father had changed his whole attitude toward her. She was no longer his great pet. He accused her of worrying her mother and disappointing him. No matter what she did, he took the worst view.

It is a bit soul-destroying, Lucinda thought with youthful dramatic emotion. *I don't really deserve my reputation. Maybe if this is found out, Mummy and Daddy will hear and I'll be for it. But it will get back on Zoë. I can't resist it!*

Vivian was now saying in so many words: '*I dare you*'. The fatal challenge Cindy could never resist.

"Let's get a paper and pencil and draw a plan of the rooms. You show me exactly what I've got to do," she said, eyes sparkling at Vivian.

Vivian laughed softly to herself. Good! Things were going just as she hoped.

Lucinda did not know that Zoë had asked this morning to be moved into a less noisy room at the back of the hotel. Cindy wouldn't have the least idea who *would* be sleeping in that front bedroom when she 'burgled it' tonight.

But Vivian knew. . . .

3

LUCINDA deftly and noiselessly climbed over her balcony and on to the adjoining balcony. Darkness and silence prevailed over the Alexandra Hotel. The day of rain and wind had settled down to a dry night, but it was moonless. Lucinda used to boast that because her mother had made her eat so many carrots she could see at night; 'Cat's Eyes Cindy', they called her at school because she had embarked on many such escapades. And now it was the reckless, mischievous child of the past rather than the eighteen-year-old young woman of today who carried out the plan made with Vivian Brill-Burrie. She half regretted her decision, but having begun went on with it.

She had put on black, tight-fitting slacks, rope-soled sandals, which she wore on the beach, and a high-necked black sweater. In this attire she had a lithe, boyish grace. When she had looked at herself in the mirror just now she had thought, sardonically:

"I only need a stocking over my face and I'd be a real 'hold-up' girl!"

Over another wrought-iron balustrade—then third window along to Zoë's room.

During dinner tonight, Zoë once again flashed her diamonds and had looked thoroughly over-dressed for an English seaside hotel. Vivian's gaze had caught Lucinda's. The latter had winked at her. Yes, it was time someone taught Zoë a lesson.

Lucinda crept noiselessly through the open windows of Zoë's bedroom.

She stepped lightly into the big well-furnished room which was darkened by heavy curtains of quilted chintz. She could but faintly discern the outline of a recumbent form in the bed. She tiptoed toward it.

Now for The Big Moment.

Lucinda laid a hand on the sleeper's face.

"Wakey, wakey! Your jewellery or your life," she giggled, and began to hum under her breath that catchy tune from *Kismet*: *Bangles, bangles, bangles and beads . . . I want 'em all.* Then she stopped. Her heart gave the strangest lurch. For her slim finger-tips were stroking, not the smooth cheek of Mrs. Ennerman but the stubbles of a *beard*.

She couldn't have come through the wrong window. She *couldn't*. This was the third room along. This *was* Zoë's room.

Lucinda stifled a scream. At that moment the figure on the bed sat upright. A hand reached out. The bedroom was flooded with light from the bedside lamp. Cindy's startled eyes, wide with horror, looked not into Mrs. Ennerman's face but *the face of Wilfred Brill-Burrie*.

He stared back at her, his hands gripping the sides of the bed, looking a trifle ludicrous with his tousled hair and gaping mouth.

"Oh, *crumbs!*" Lucinda muttered and turned to dart away but the doctor sprang from his bed and seized her wrists.

"Oh no, you don't. Come back. What does this mean?"

For an instant she was completely at a loss for an answer. She did not know whether to giggle or burst into tears. She had had a real fright. Serve her right, she told herself. She should never have embarked on such a stupid adventure, even though Vivian had encouraged it.

Vivian's husband manoeuvred himself into the foulard dressing-gown which was flung over the bottom of his bed. Angry, startled out of a deep sleep, he stared with unbelieving eyes at this young girl.

"What the hell's going on?" he demanded. "What are you doing in my room?" he added, as he glanced at his bedside clock. "Two in the morning. Are you out of your mind?"

Cindy put a hand up to her lips.

"Oh, gosh, I thought . . . I didn't dream *you* were in here . . ." she stuttered and stopped.

He glowered. That was possibly true. It was only this afternoon that he had moved into this room and Zoë had vacated it. When he had first arrived he had asked for two communicating rooms with his wife but they hadn't been available and she hated a double room, so they'd stuck him in one at the back. He had made a fuss and the manager had told him that he should have the first front room that came vacant. That was why he was here.

He looked suspiciously at Cindy.

"You're sure you didn't *know* I was in here?"

She burst into laughter.

"How can you be so silly?"

Now he felt angry. He caught both her wrists. He said:

"My dear, you need a firm hand and I'm going to give you a lecture. If you go on behaving in this silly, childish way you'll get yourself into one helluva mess one day. I'm sure you *don't* mean any harm but other men might take advantage."

He added more to this. Lucinda bit her lip. She had begun to find the situation less amusing but she wasn't going to show it.

"Oh, don't be so stuffy, Wilfred——" she began.

He interrupted and she suddenly felt the fun was really over. She wanted to get out. But it was too late. The door opened.

Vivian, her dark hair unbound, flowing around her neck, marched in. She was followed by the portly figure of Lucinda's godmother.

"There you are!" exclaimed Vivian loudly. "You see, Lady Hordham, I *told* you your charming god-daughter was having an affair with my husband. Now I've caught them red-handed. You can witness the fact."

If ever a pair looked guilty, and without justification, it was Wilfred and Lucinda. They were both pulverised, and stood there dumbly staring at their accuser.

Cindy felt as though a bomb had exploded and it was a bomb that *she* had set off, she thought in acute dismay. But surely Vivian couldn't be saying these terrible things. Vivian had suggested this adventure. But Lucinda read only a strange triumph in Vivian's eyes. Lady Hordham, her waved hair under a net, her face greasy with nourishing cream, her mouth sagging with shocked horror, was the next to speak.

"Well, I never! I just can't *believe* it."

"You have to. You can see for yourself what goes on," said Vivian. "I've expected it ever since we got here. Wilfred's been a snake-in-the-grass, acting as he always does like the meek, too-good-to-live husband, henpecked by his wife. The boot's on the other foot. It's Wilfred who has led me a frightful life and made me a wreck. I couldn't sleep tonight. I came along to ask Wilfred for some tablets. I heard Lucinda's voice. I made you, Lady Hordham, get up and come with me. I had a key, Wilfred *forgot* that. Now it's the *end*, Wilfred . . ." she addressed herself to her flabbergasted husband. "I shall divorce you and cite that girl as co-respondent in the case."

The doctor pulled himself together. Scarlet in the face, he said:

"You must be out of your mind, Vivian."

She began to weep.

"You cruel, heartless man. *You*, a doctor, having an affair with a young girl, too. I suppose you wanted youth. I'm too old for you; you've been indifferent to my suffering for *ages*!"

"Wait a minute . . ." began Lady Hordham. "Just *one* moment. Let me speak . . ."

"No, let *me* speak," Lucinda said suddenly. She was strangely calm now. "I want you to know that I believed this was Zoë Ennerman's bedroom."

Vivian's voice cut like a whiplash.

"Oh, now—you knew perfectly well that my husband had moved in here. Besides, you've even admitted to me that my husband was always pursuing you. Everyone has remarked on the way you have behaved with *him*."

Lucinda, shocked, stared at the woman she had thought her

friend. It was as though she saw something she had thought attractive and harmless, change before her eyes into a poisonous snake. She broke out:

"But that's an infamous lie, Vivian. You know perfectly well we thought this up together . . . it was to be a joke—it was because of Zoë's jewellery . . ." her voice trailed away.

Vivian sniffed into her handkerchief and moved toward the door.

"*You* pretending to be so innocent and going behind my back like this, my heart is absolutely broken."

She ran sobbing from the room.

Mary Hordham was not a clever woman, neither was she very quick-witted. She was kindly and rather stupid. She, too, began to cry.

"Oh dear, oh dear, what *will* your mother say, Cindy. What shall we do? You silly, *silly* girl!"

"But it's not what you think. I tell you this was all a joke and Mrs. Brill-Burrie instigated it. She didn't tell me her husband was in here," said Lucinda in a suffocated voice.

She still could not believe that Vivian had struck at her so treacherously. She was, herself, far too honest and guileless to imagine there could be such evil in the world.

"Lady Hordham," Wilfred said, addressing the older woman, "I assure you Cindy and I have *not* been having a love affair. Cindy is quite right when she tells you that."

Lady Hordham sniffed into her handkerchief.

"If you'll forgive my saying so, Dr. Brill-Burrie, I think your wife has said some very alarming things, and even if she can't actually pin this thing on Cindy, she can create a terrible scandal. But do you think she really *means* to try and divorce you and involve Cindy?"

"I don't know," said Wilfred. His own heart felt leaden—weighed down by the most alarming possibilities. He knew Vivian better than any of them; was well aware of the lengths to which she might go. For a long time, of course, she had been wanting evidence for a divorce.

Lucinda trembled. What had started as a gay escapade had ended as a nightmare.

"Aunt Mary," she said, "I know I've got a silly reputation but I'm not *bad*. Oh, you know I'm not."

"But you two *were* in here together . . ." began Lady Hordham, sobbing. "Oh, dear, of course I'll try to believe you and do all I can to help, but if Mrs. Brill-Burrie really means to bring an action against her husband, it's bound to ruin you. You, my god-daughter . . ." she began to cry again in earnest. "And while I was chaperoning you, too. What *will* your parents say to me!"

Lucinda stared from her godmother to the doctor.

"You won't let this happen, will you?" she said. She suddenly looked very young and frightened.

He was in a state of shock but he knew in his heart that this girl was guileless. It appalled him to think that his own wife could have perpetrated such a wicked scheme and at such a cost to an eighteen-year-old girl.

"Of course I'll try and make my wife see sense," he said.

Lady Hordham led Lucinda from the room. She was sure Mrs. Brill-Burrie would never carry out her intentions, she said. Everything would be all right in the morning.

Lucinda went back to her own room. She lay on top of her bed in her dressing-gown until daylight—too upset to sleep.

Soon after eight o'clock Lady Hordham came in to see her.

"Well, you might as well know the worst," she said looking white and worried. "Dr. and Mrs. Brill-Burrie packed up early and have already left the hotel."

"Oh, my *goodness*," muttered Cindy.

"Yes," went on Lady Hordham. "I didn't see Vivian but I saw *him*. He said that he'd been arguing with his wife half the night but she refused to believe he was not having an affair with you and she does intend to drag you into a divorce. Of course she hasn't really a leg to stand on and he says she will never get any solicitor to take the case. There isn't enough evidence. But it'll mean a public scandal. You really *have* got yourself into a fix this time, Lucinda."

The girl, heavy-eyed, white, drew in her breath.

"But Aunt Mary, it isn't *true*. I've never had an affair with Wilfred. It's fantastically stupid. Why, I wouldn't let him touch me with the end of a barge-pole."

"Maybe, but it's quite plain to me that Mrs. Brill-Burrie is all out for trouble. My own impression now is that she is not as hard done by as she liked us to believe and has been having an affair of her own so she wants her freedom, and this is the way she decided to get it. I'm very disillusioned. I thought she was so sweet."

"So did I," said Lucinda, bitterly.

But she could see that she could not minimise the danger in which she now found herself. Before another hour passed, she realised that the unspeakable Vivian's treachery had started the rot . . . the rot that was to spread deeply into Lucinda's young life. By breakfast-time the whole hotel seemed to know about the nocturnal episode which had ended in the early departure of Dr. and Mrs. Brill-Burrie. Even Tommy Marchent goggled at his happy 'playmate' of yesterday.

"I *say*, Cindy! . . . Why didn't you climb over *my* balcony, honey-chile? You chose the wrong chap . . ."

She turned on him like a wild-cat.

"How awful of you! You know perfectly well I didn't deliberately pay the doctor a visit. I thought it was Zoë Ennerman's bedroom . . . I was pretending to be a cat-burglar after her diamonds."

And that was what Lucinda kept on saying again and again whenever she was tackled. That was what she told her parents when at length they confronted her.

Lucinda packed up and left the Alexandra Hotel with her godmother. The holiday, which was to have been such fun, came to an abrupt end. The family attacked Lucinda soundly once they were all together in the small but pleasant lounge of the Mace home in Putney. For once the prettiness was wiped from Lucinda's face. Her eyes were red from weeping, her hair was untidy and her young face drawn. She stood like a creature at bay, answering the questions put to her, repeating again and again:

"I never had an affair with the doctor. It's absolutely ridiculous. I thought it was Zoë's bedroom."

Angela Mace wept silently, her handkerchief pressed against her lips. She believed implicitly in her daughter's innocence. Arthur Mace, Cindy's father, a big man with a bald head and glasses, and a bombastic nature, exploded, heckled and alternated between believing Cindy and doubting her. As he told her, this wasn't the first time her name had been linked with some boy's, only she had always avoided serious trouble and they all knew that her fun was innocent enough. But she had been warned again and again to pull herself together and behave like a sensible adult and get away from that reckless sensation-hunting set of hers.

"I don't care whether you deliberately visited this fellow or thought it was some woman's bedroom," Mr. Mace said loudly. "You must have been playing up in some way or other to make Mrs. Brill-Burrie suspect you so far that she entered her husband's bedroom, with Lady Hordham as a witness. Poor little Mrs. Brill-Burrie," he said, "such a lovely little thing and so frail. The fellow ought to be horse-whipped for making her so unhappy."

"How can you defend her?" asked Lucinda, wildly. "She's just taken you in like she took me. She's *vile* under all that frailty and sadness she wraps herself in."

Mr. Mace glowered at his young daughter. She had been born late in his life. He had been over forty when the little girl came along. They had spoiled her. This was the result. In this hour, all affection for her was swallowed up in a wave of righteous indignation. Not only did Mr. Mace feel the thing because of *her* reputation, but his own. He was a respected man in Putney, a Jobber on the Stock Exchange, a personal friend of the Vicar's, and warden of the church. If this got into the papers, it would be *most* unpleasant.

Lucinda looked from one to the other of the three people who counted most in her life. Mother, father, godmother . . . all against her, she thought bitterly, even though they said they weren't and that they wanted to protect her. *But they didn't really believe she was guiltless.* That was what shook Cindy to the foundations. At first she had been bitterly distressed and ashamed. Now with greater bitterness she resented all the cruelty of injustice. But too late she realised that she was the victim of her own stupidity. Till now she had been dancing through life adoring the champagne froth. Nobody knew that deep in her heart she had meant to 'grow-up' one day soon. She had fully intended to settle down and find real love.

She heard her father's pompous voice.

"It's obvious we're living in times when young people think they know best and get into dire trouble because of it."

She turned on him.

"How can you take Vivian Brill-Burrie's part against *me*, your own daughter?"

"Yes, how?" murmured Mrs. Mace, a trifle darkly.

"Of course," said Mr. Mace, climbing down, "I'll believe you, Cindy. It may only have been an innocent escapade but Mrs. Brill-Burrie, poor little woman, must have reason to suspect her husband. She just happens to be pinning this on to you. What we've got to do now is to try and clear your name and that won't be easy."

Lucinda turned and went out of the room. She had been through enough. She refused to come out of her room for the rest of that day.

Later that afternoon, Mary Hordham telephoned her friend, Angela, with news calculated to depress the Mace family still further.

She had tried to see Vivian Brill-Burrie several times, she

said, but failed. She had left her own home and, according to her husband, was staying with a married sister in Hampstead. The determined Lady Hordham had ferreted out the telephone number there but received a cold reply from the sister to say that 'poor little Vivian was prostrate and would see and speak to nobody'. When Lady Hordham had mentioned the incident at Oversands, the sister had said, sharply:

"I don't want to discuss it. But you can be sure Vivian will make that girl suffer. She has broken up a happy marriage."

Mrs. Mace wept afresh.

"Oh dear, what can we do?"

"Happy marriage indeed," snorted Lady Hordham. "We must continue to fight this thing, Angela. I personally intend to stand by my god-daughter through thick and thin. Even if I'm forced under oath to admit I saw her in the doctor's bedroom, I shall say I know there was nothing in it."

When Lucinda was told this she felt deeply grateful, but all the joy had gone out of life for her. She was still in a state of shock and desperately unhappy. She felt that she did not know what was true or what was false and could believe nobody. Worse was to follow. The mad yet innocent escapade was like one of those awful mushrooms, she thought with a shudder, rising from a single bomb but spreading its poison for hundreds of miles. *Vivian* was the mushroom. She made it evident, too, during the weeks that followed that she was going to hit at Lucinda with every weapon she could find—without respect for honour or justice.

Lucinda woke up to the realisation that soon everybody knew about it—every friend or acquaintance in the big circle in which she and her family moved. There were one or two faithful friends who met her in the street, looked at her with embarrassed gaze but muttered, 'Of *course* we don't believe these ridiculous allegations against you, darling.'

There were the others who gave her a brief nod and hurried on. There were the unpleasant young men who rang her up and said:

"Cindy, oh *Cindy*! What about a nice crawl over the balcony in *my* direction . . .?"

Such things as that reduced her to tears and a feeling of deep mortification.

There was even one righteous, smug lady in the district, mother of an eighteen-year-old girl who had often played tennis with Cindy, who met Cindy out shopping and coldly told her that Elizabeth was sorry she couldn't play in the next tournament with her as she was going away.

Lucinda went home, hot with resentment, fully realising that her friendship with Elizabeth had been cut short because Mum 'had heard'. All the sympathy was for poor, frail little Mrs. Brill-Burrie. The fingers of scorn pointed at the girl who had 'led the doctor on'.

And the doctor, himself, was not finding the situation too easy. Lucinda heard that he, too, had cancellations—and the other sort of client who consulted him just to be thoroughly inquisitive about his broken marriage, and Cindy Mace.

Came the day when Lucinda delivered an ultimatum to her parents at breakfast-time.

"I've been thinking things over," she said. "I suppose I've only myself to blame for all this awfulness because I've been so thoughtless in the past. Now I've certainly been given something to think about. You may as well know, Mummy and Daddy, that I went to see Aunt Mary yesterday and suggested she should help me go abroad—get right away from Putney and from this beastly gossip. Then I decided that would be cowardly so instead I asked her to find me a job. I'm going to work. And I'm going to stay in London and show all these cats that I'm not afraid *because I'm not guilty*. And I refuse to behave as though I'm guilty."

Her voice trembled away. But she stood there, her back very straight, her chin well up. Her parents looked at her in silence. Mr. Mace, who had been personally most affronted by the whole business, felt a sudden revival of the deep love he used to bear his only daughter. He had always been a proud man himself and he was thrilled now by Lucinda's pride and show of courage.

"I must say I approve," he said, and coughed and adjusted his spectacles.

But Mrs. Mace was reduced to tears. She was rather a tearful sort of woman and over-sentimental. It broke her heart to see Lucinda looking so white and hollow-eyed and changed. The child had lost weight, even in these few weeks. She looked a mere ghost of the radiant, laughing Cindy who had gone down to the seaside for that fatal holiday. What a thing to have happened to her, and the poor lamb only nineteen next week. Yes, it was her birthday on Tuesday, but there was to be no party. She wouldn't hear of it.

She had suddenly grown old, the mother thought. The tennis racquets had been put away. She refused any stray invitations sent by her more kindly and charitable friends. Mrs. Mace had also noticed a strange, new orderliness in Cindy's bedroom; it was Cindy who offered to do the washing-up and the housework when the 'daily' couldn't come. She was even learning to cook—a thing she had always hated. But when Mrs. Mace was in the kitchen these days, Cindy followed her about, gravely watching. Now she told them that she was going to work for her living. Aunt Mary had found her a job in a big Knightsbridge dress-shop where her ladyship was *persona grata* because she spent a small fortune there. They were going to train Cindy to show clothes. She had beauty and intelligence, they said, and all she needed was experience.

"But I know I need more than that," said Lucinda biting her lip. "I need to learn how to keep my head screwed on and not to think life's just a bowl of cherries——" She broke off with a short, unhappy laugh.

"Oh dear," said Mrs. Mace, weakly.

Cindy walked round the table and put her arms around her mother's neck.

"Sorry, Mum. I'm afraid I've caused you a lot of trouble."

The doorbell rang.

"I'll go," said Mr. Mace. "I think it's the garage about the car."

But it was not. It was Wilfred Brill-Burrie. Hastily, Mr. Mace announced this to the family.

"I don't want to see him," began Cindy passionately, but subsided. "I suppose I'd better," she added in a whisper.

They all gathered in the lounge. Wilfred, hat in hand, looked at the young girl with embarrassment, and then turned gloomily to her parents.

"I thought I ought to come personally and let you know," he said, "that I've managed after a lot of difficulty to have a meeting with my wife in the presence of my solicitor and hers."

Cindy went cold then the colour flamed into her cheeks. Her mother gripped her by the hand and pressed it encouragingly. It was her father who spoke:

"Well, and with what result? Is this ridiculous divorce going on? Is my daughter to be implicated?"

4

"No," answered Wilfred. "There is to be no divorce—at least not for the moment. If and when it comes, it will not be on account of that absurd trumped-up affair at the Alexandra Hotel."

Outsize relief surged into Cindy's heart. For a moment she was struck dumb. She could only stare at her parents, flicking her lashes against the hot tears. Mrs. Mace spoke:

"Well, I'm *very* thankful to hear this, Dr. Brill-Burrie. And it's only right. We have never believed for a moment that Cindy did wrong and she should never have been implicated in such an abominable way."

Mr. Mace loudly agreed. He, too, was vastly relieved—his mind firmly fixed on his daughter's reputation, his own, the club and the office. For nights he had sweated at the thought of the name Mace being dragged through the courts. Pages in the Sunday papers. Shocking reports with Cindy's photograph and *somehow*, he fully believed, those devils in Fleet Street would have got hold of a photograph of Cindy in a swim-suit, rather than a respectable dress, and published it with a mischievous caption. She would have been *ruined*.

Wilfred stood twiddling his hat between nervous fingers.

"It's all been very unpleasant. It's still very grim for me," he said. "But at least Vivian was convinced after talking to the lawyers that she would never get away with her case because of lack of important evidence. It has to have more to it than just a girl in jeans and jersey being found in a man's bedroom —even in the early hours of the morning."

Now Cindy blinked away her tears. She flung back her head with a proud, resentful movement.

"It makes me sick—the whole thing makes me *sick*!" she said, choking.

"Calm down, darling. It's all right now," whispered her mother.

"But I don't know that it is!" argued Cindy. "I bet Vivian has told absolutely everybody in the district, *and* more besides. You know we've already had *proof* of that. Nobody will believe I'm innocent."

Wilfred eyed the girl gloomily. He was a kind man by disposition and although immensely harassed by his personal relationship with the wife who had so foully accused him, his main feeling was of anger on Cindy's behalf. It wasn't fair that she should have been made to suffer on account of a childish prank—no, she had behaved like a little fool and needed what he called 'a touch of the stick', but there was no real harm in her. He, of all men, knew that. But of course she was right, people would gossip. Vivian had told everybody her lies. And quite a number of people believed her. With all that sweetness and pathos Vivian was so well able to muster, using her delicacy as an infallible weapon, she had enlisted universal sympathy. Her own sister had rung Wilfred up and dressed him down in terms that had scorched him.

Brute . . . monster . . . a dirty dog playing about with a young girl, when his ailing wife, older than himself, was laid up. Vivian, poor little thing, tortured by migraine, going into his bedroom at the hotel and finding the girl there. And he had always been unfaithful . . . Vivian had told her sister so. Poor darling Vivian!

All Wilfred's denials could not stem the ugly flow of accusations, nor wash from Lucinda and himself the mire Vivian had spread. It would stick—for a long time. He knew enough about life, its cruelties and injustices to realise *that*.

"I'm clearing out of England," at length he said in a harsh, loud voice. "I've had enough of my married life here and I can see that my practice won't be of much value to me. Everybody in Putney loves dear, sweet, badly treated little Vivian and believes that Lucinda and I . . ."

He broke off, wiping his lips with his handkerchief, his hands trembling.

Lucinda went scarlet. The Maces stared. They could see that the doctor was in a sorry state. They were sorry for him. But they were sorrier for their daughter. Kind, anxious to help though he was, this man's name was irrefutably linked with Lucinda's. They were glad he was going abroad. They wanted to be rid of him. The sooner the better.

Wilfred did not stay. He had little more to say. At Lucinda he barely glanced except as he left he held out a hand to her.

"Please forgive me for what my wife has done to you. I wouldn't have had it happen for anything in the world."

Now her soft heart stirred with pity. She placed her cold, slender fingers in his for the fraction of a moment.

"I wish you luck, wherever you go, doctor. And I'm the one who ought to say 'Sorry'. It was my fault. I was mad ever to play that stupid joke. It seems so ironic that Vivian and I planned it together and I thought it would be such fun to teach Zoë not to flash her diamonds around."

The doctor squeezed the small cold hand, then let it drop. He sighed heavily.

"Ironic is hardly the word," he said. "The whole thing was an abomination. Vivian wanted her freedom and thought that would be the way to get it. And the amazing thing is that she's still playing her 'little angel' game and getting away with it. Nobody can pin anything on *her*, of course. She's been too careful. But that's my funeral. I'll go now. I have an elder brother living in Tasmania. I shall try and get out there and start a new life. I repeat that if there's to be a divorce between Vivian and myself—it will have nothing whatsoever to do with you, Lucinda."

Then he was gone. Mrs. Mace gave a sigh of relief.

"That's over, we've nothing more to fear."

I expect I have, the thought leapt into Lucinda's mind. I expect for a long time all this scandal around me will linger— and spread just like ripples when somebody has thrown a stone into still water.

"We really ought to move——" began Mrs. Mace.

Here Lucinda interrupted.

"Once and for all, Mummy, *no*. I'm not going to run away. I'm taking this job in Knightsbridge and I'm going to show everybody that I am not afraid of beastly gossip."

Mrs. Mace dried her eyes and patted her daughter's shoulder.

"You're a brave girl, I must say."

"One has to be a bit brave to get through life, Mummy."

"Oh dear, I hate to hear you make such a cynical remark at your age."

Lucinda walked to the window and stared out.

"I'm not a child any more," she said in a low voice. "I've grown up, Mummy."

But the process of growing up proved to be painful for her in more ways than one. The sly looks, the wagging tongues, and the falling off in the number of friends who used to visit the Maces, continued for a long time. Funny, Lucinda thought, that even now when everybody was supposed to be so broad-minded, there was still a strong Puritan streak running through the nice, ordinary, respectable families who lived round about, who gathered at the Tennis Club, or exchanged visits. Broad-minded they might be about the sort of things they read in the daily papers or the broad jokes they heard in plays and films and on television. But when it came down to facts, the *nice* mothers of *nice* daughters wanted the *niceness* to prevail. So many who had known the Brill-Burries had had the wool pulled across their eyes by 'Poor little Vivian'. And whether Cindy was guilty in every sense of the word or not, she *had* been found in that doctor's bedroom in the early hours of the morning, they said. And one *couldn't* altogether believe that silly story about her not knowing whose room it was . . . after all Lucinda Mace *had* earned a reputation for herself for being a *very* Bright Young Thing.

So, for Cindy there began a trying time. There were moments when her courage flagged and her depression was such that she almost wished she had accepted her mother's offer to send her abroad, or take her right away from this place where everybody knew her. Then pride would reassert itself.

"I am not going to run away as though I was guilty. I am *not!*" she would keep saying both to herself and her dubious mother.

Her friend Iris stood by her, as a true friend would. Iris knew Cindy so well.

"I've never heard such a lot of tripe as *your* having a desperate affair with that old osteopath. It's *rot!*" she had said.

And Iris had tolerant, amiable parents who were not as ready as some to believe the worst of Cindy. There was always a corner for Cindy in the Turnbull household. There were others like the Turnbulls too, of course, and the indomitable Lady Hordham who stood by her god-daughter from start to finish.

Through Lady Hordham, Cindy heard that Dr. Brill-Burrie left Putney some three months later. Nobody quite knew where he had gone. Some said to his brother in Tasmania. Somebody else thought Canada. Anyhow, as far as Cindy could judge he had gone right out of her life.

As for Vivian, she, too, was thought to have left England and gone abroad. It was later rumoured that a divorce had taken place and that Vivian had married again. Possibly, Lucinda thought, to the man with the big car who used to take her out at Oversands. Cindy didn't know and didn't care. As she told Iris one day, she could only think of Vivian as 'something that had crawled out from under a stone'.

Now Lucinda's whole personality seemed to change. She stuck grimly to her decision to remain in the old circle and keep her head held high. Gradually, of course, the gossip died down. Everyone had their own lives to lead and Cindy was soon left in peace to lead hers. She was thankful that Vivian had not had the power to hurt her more. In time, the harm that had been done to Cindy seemed to crystallise into good. The feckless, over-exuberant child of eighteen entered her twentieth year like a small, rudderless ship that had learned to ride the waters with steady dignity. She did well on the staff at Ruchelle. The proprietor liked her and Madame Colette, the manageress, relied on her. That was what really pleased Cindy. She had begun to take her place in life as a reliable person. And there came a day when she also proved herself more than an ordinarily devoted daughter.

Things went wrong at home.

Mr. Mace came up against bad times. For many men on the Stock Exchange it had been a boom period. But not for him. He arrived one day to tell his wife and daughter that he was on the verge of a financial collapse. They would all have to cut down. If it wasn't that they were living in a house they had bought years ago at a cheap price and couldn't hope to find anything cheaper in these days of exorbitant rents, they would have left Putney. But it must mean rigid economy. No more entertaining. No domestic help. Angela Mace, like so many women of her calibre, showed up at her best at a time like this. Instead of weeping and whining, now she put on an overall and turned herself into both cook and 'daily'. Lucinda made her own contribution. She showed how grateful she was to the mother and father who had kept faith in her when things had looked so black. Three-quarters of her salary went into the house-keeping. And when in the autumn of that year her mother showed signs of considerable fatigue, Lucinda came home from her job and cooked the evening meal. Week-ends were no longer spent among young people of her own age. She took on quite a lot of responsibility. She spent money on her own clothes and make-up only when they were necessary. She generally managed to find a cheap, shop-soiled model—helped by the kindly Madame Colette.

Once her mother looked at her sadly.

"Oh, darling," she said. "You're getting *so* much too serious. Sometimes I miss my gay little giggling school-girl."

"Well I *don't* miss her. She's dead and gone so far as I'm concerned," was Lucinda's reply.

"You must have fun sometimes, darling."

"I do have fun in my way. We're all good friends at Ruchelle and I go out with Iris, don't I?"

"But it's time you had a boy friend——" began Mrs. Mace.

Cindy broke in, colouring.

"I don't feel very interested in boys these days."

"But Cindy, you're getting on for twenty-one. You ought to——"

Again the girl interrupted.

"I haven't met the right man yet. I'm not in a hurry, Mum."

And she was not. But the day came when the inevitable happened. She went to a party at the Turnbulls, and there it was that Derek Chalmerson—the young bio-chemist—came into her life. Once she knew that she loved this fair, clean-limbed, integral young man, and that she was loved by him in return, she felt her cup of happiness to be full. She felt almost humble about it too, as though she had no right to be so happy because once she had been such a fool.

Then started the queer, uneasy wondering as to whether Derek would ever hear about the Brill-Burrie affair. And *if* he did, how he would react. He was not particularly tolerant in his outlook—she knew that. Perhaps that was his one besetting fault, although she could find few others. Besides, she didn't think it a bad thing for a boy to have strong principles. So many these days had none. She wanted passionately to live up to Derek's ideal.

It was the most wonderful Christmas she had spent since the complete reversal of her fortunes. But there came a moment of peril which shook her considerably.

It was on the very night of the Turnbulls' Christmas-Eve party where she and Derek were guests.

It was during the buffet supper. She and Derek had just been pulling crackers and arranging paper caps on each other's heads with the usual childish abandon indulged in by adults at

Christmas. Suddenly a middle-aged woman came up and introduced herself, cheerfully. She was a Mrs. Curry. She had just arrived from Tasmania, she said. She was on a visit to an aged father who lived in Putney and was a distant cousin of Mrs. Turnbull's. Derek went off for a moment. The two women were alone. Lucinda looked at Mrs. Curry a trifle bleakly. That word *Tasmania* had rung an unpleasant bell. It carried her back to Wilfred Brill-Burrie, who had a brother out there. It was long since she had allowed herself to worry actively about him or Vivian. But it all recurred tonight with a horrid jolt. Mrs. Curry was voluble. Chatter, *chatter*. And suddenly, up came the name Cindy had dreaded to hear.

"We had a Putney man come out to Tasmania. You may know him. An osteopath, Dr. Brill-Burrie. As a matter of fact, he wasn't a great success and I believe he has moved since, to the Cape now. He was rather an unhappy creature. People found him a bit of a bore. I wonder if you ever knew him?"

Lucinda drew in her breath.

"Yes, I knew him."

Mrs. Curry dropped her voice to a confidential whisper.

"He was divorced, wasn't he? They say some bit of a girl here in the locality was the cause. She broke up what had been a very happy marriage. Did you know her?"

The golden world of Christmas candles, the glittering frosted tree hung with coloured balls and gaily wrapped presents, the radio playing and the sight of all the young dancing, went hazy before Lucinda's sight. She saw Derek striding back in her direction. And suddenly she said under her breath:

"*No, I didn't know her.*"

Then she turned her back on the woman from Tasmania and hurried to meet Derek. Her heart was thumping. She didn't know it was possible that she could have been dragged back so sharply to a past that she had hoped was dead. A bitter, choking resentment drained all the colour from her face.

He was divorced . . . some bit of a girl . . . the cause . . . Oh, beastly, unjust, *untrue.*

Derek took Lucinda's arm. He looked fondly down at her. She was glorious, this girl with the chestnut hair and grave, sweet eyes, and that lemon-coloured chiffon evening dress suited her slenderness so charmingly. He found her enchanting.

"You look as though you'd seen a spook," he murmured. "Anything wrong?"

"No," she said under her breath. "Nothing. But perhaps I *did* see a ghost just now."

"I didn't know this house was haunted," he laughed.

"Neither did I," she said.

She got as far away from Mrs. Curry as she could.

She *felt* haunted for the rest of the evening. But Mrs. Curry obviously had no great interest in the gossip about Dr. Brill-Burrie, and obviously didn't repeat it because nobody said anything to Cindy, neither did the woman seem to know the name of the 'young girl' of the Brill-Burrie story.

But that night when Derek kissed her, Cindy prayed quite extravagantly that such a horrid coincidence would never be repeated and that that particular ghost would never be raised again. Certainly not for Derek to see. He, of all men, must never know about her past.

5

MAX CHALMERSON did not drink champagne. He chose gin-and-tonic, which he preferred. He, too, examined a large menu, cigarette between his fine, nervous fingers. But his mind was not on the tempting names on the *plat-de-jour* or *à la carte*. His gaze kept wandering to the young girl who was sitting beside his half-brother. In fact, he was taking stock of both of them.

Derek never changed, he thought. Nice kid. Max was fond of him—in an elder-brotherly way. Being older and so much more worldly-wise and widely travelled, he could rarely look on things on quite the same eye-level as Derek, who had always been just the 'kid' to him. Physically, Derek was the counterpart of his own mother. Daphne Chalmerson had had the same bright hair and pink-and-white colouring. Poor little step-mama, thought Max with a sigh. He had been fond of her. She had died with tragic suddenness in Borneo where Dr. Chalmerson, who had fathered both Max and Derek—and was a great expert on tropical diseases—had been working at the time. Max's mother had been different—a strong, silent woman from whom Max had inherited his dark hair and light grey eyes. He remembered, too, that she had been tall and strong. Her death had been accidental—she was thrown from a horse riding in Rhodesia, from which country she originated.

Dr. Chalmerson had been the sort of man who never could stay at home but travelled from one dark continent to the other and took his wife with him. Poor little Daphne had not survived her small son's eighth birthday. Both the boys had been sent back to England to boarding school. As far back as he could remember, Max had been in charge of Derek and developed that special affection that an elder brother often lavishes on a younger, more delicate one.

Before death finally came to Dr. Chalmerson, Max had given his solemn promise that he would look after young Derry. The fair little boy had been his father's favourite but Max had no jealousy in his make-up and it had never entered his head to feel one spark of it. Derek, showing a prowess for maths and chemistry, had kept to that line—hence his present job. But Max was his father over again. Restless, with an essential need to explore—to discover and to benefit humanity if possible. During the last few years he had been in the employ of the Ministry of Agriculture and Fisheries. His last job was that of game warden in his mother's country. Then he had been sent with a Government Board of Inquiry to Kenya to deal with welfare of wild animals in the Game Reserves. It was this work that interested him most and on which he was working when Derek flew out to him for a holiday last year.

When, a few weeks ago, he received Derek's first enthusiastic letter about his sudden engagement to a young London girl named Lucinda Mace, Max was delighted. He had often thought it would be a good thing for Derry to marry. He was the reserved, home-loving type and he had really never had a home, poor little brute. He would make an ideal husband. (At least, Max supposed he would from the woman's viewpoint.) He was sure Derek would be domesticated and faithful and never put a wrong foot forward. That was his temperament. But Max had to admit in the depths of his heart that at times *he*, personally, found Derek a bit of a bore. He was a little *too* correct. Max had sometimes tried to laugh him out of it.

"Don't get too smug, young Derry," he used to say. "Stick to your principles but remember that tolerance is the finest quality anyone can develop. You *must* always be tolerant of other people's likes and dislikes and failings."

But Max could never be quite sure that Derek knew the meaning of the word tolerance.

Here, however, was the lad's chance to settle down with a wife and family. And when Max was told by his Chief that for the moment his job was at an end and he could return to

England on long leave, he had seized the opportunity to fly home in time for Derek's engagement party. He was enormously interested to meet his future sister-in-law and hopeful that Derek had made the right choice.

If he had built up any sort of mental picture of Lucinda, it was of a rather strait-laced 'nice little thing' who would suit Derek's rather exacting taste.

And then . . . Vivian Brill-Burrie had told him about Lucinda.

Amazing coincidence that Vivian should have entered his life and so been able to give him the warning. Damned worrying, too. What Vivian had had to say had dampened Max's ardent hopes that Derry had found the right girl. It was quite obvious that he was pinning his faith on the wrong one and that he was completely ignorant of the sort of person she really was.

This had given Max a double incentive to get home before things went too far. For if it was going to be at all possible for him to stop Derry from making a complete fool of himself, Max meant to do so. It had hitherto been his policy not to interfere with other people's lives, but with Derek it was different. There was that promise to their father that he would look after him and Max was going to do it.

The Max who sat in the Savoy tonight, his gaze moving from Derek to Lucinda and back again, was not altogether a happy man. He felt thoroughly awkward about the whole situation.

Derry looks so damned pleased with himself—as usual. I wish this hadn't happened, Max kept thinking.

His eyes also turned to the dance floor and to the attractive woman in red who smiled and waved at him every time she passed the table.

Max first met Vivian at a party in Nairobi two or three months ago. She had told him that she had divorced her husband and was living with cousins in Kenya. Max met her several times afterwards. He found her quite charming and felt rather sorry for her. He was one of those big, physically very strong men who invariably feel moved to pity for some-body very small and delicate like Vivian. Quite apart from the fact that she had very beautiful amber-coloured eyes, she seemed so pathetic. She said that she had had a ghastly time— once married to an osteopath whom she had adored until some unspeakable girl had broken up her marriage. Max, after listening to her story, had said at the time:

"If there's one type I have no use for, it's the sort of girl who comes between husband and wife. It shows a complete lack of scruples—quite unforgivable. A girl can't always help falling for a married man but she should keep away from him— especially when the wife is older. It's all so damned unfair."

And Derek's fiancée was the girl.

Max and Vivian had been sitting in the bar of one of the big hotels in Nairobi having a drink together one evening after Max returned from visiting the Tanganyika border.

He had been camping under Kilimanjaro. It was the sort of work he worshipped—living with men who like himself understood wild animals and life in the African Bush. Men who, like himself, found life trivial in the city compared with the enormity of adventure in the wild, wide spaces, far away from civilisation. It was this spirit which had perhaps kept Max so far from tying himself up in marriage. He wanted to remain free—a bachelor—until he was at least thirty-five.

Once or twice he had imagined himself in love. Without un-due conceit he knew that he attracted women. He was always being told by them that he had both looks and charm. Perhaps his very unwillingness to be drawn into the 'net' made him all the more of a challenge. But so far he had escaped. It had soon become of course plain to him that Vivian Brill-Burrie was attracted by him. But there had so far been no question of 'an affair'.

Somebody—he didn't remember who—had told him out in Nairobi that she had been on the verge of remarrying after her divorce but that the boy friend had not come up to scratch. The poor little thing had had bad luck all round,

Max thought. Then when he had told her cheerfully about his half-brother's engagement and mentioned the name of the girl, Vivian had gone quite white. She had to have another strong drink before she recovered sufficiently to tell him the reason why she was affected. With a sinking heart he had listened to her story. He had no reason to doubt its authenticity.

"*Can you imagine*," she had finished, the tears glistening on her long lashes, "how awful it was for me to find Lucinda in my husband's bedroom when I thought we were such *friends*, too! And I'd done so *much* for her."

"She sounds an ungrateful little brute," Max had answered. "Only eighteen, you say? She was starting young."

Vivian had wiped her eyes and murmured:

"Just no good, I fear. I knew she had a pretty poor reputation but I used to think it was just nonsense on her part. I soon learned what she was really like. Oh, Max, you *can't* let this brother whom you say you are so fond of, marry a girl like that."

"What can I do?" Max had asked, uneasily.

"You must tell him."

"But it's some time ago it all happened."

"It doesn't matter. It's not all that long and I expect she's been dashing around the place ever since upsetting other women's lives. It's time she was stopped. Obviously she's been looking for a husband and your nice, unsuspecting brother has been caught."

Those words had made Max think. True, young Derry was just the type to be 'caught'. Max was dead certain that Derek didn't know much about Lucinda or he would never have proposed marriage to her. The brothers had sometimes discussed women and Derry had stated categorically that he would never marry the kind of girl who, as he boyishly put it, 'racketed around with men'. Not for him the ultra-modern type with loose morals or the sort to 'try it out before marriage'. To Derek, purity was an essential in the make-up of a girl.

"Poor old Derek," Max had thought after Vivian's revelation. "The poor kid—to pick on a little devil like Lucinda."

A *vendeuse* from a dress-shop. Well that hadn't worried Max when he first heard about her job. He was neither a snob nor ready to believe the worst, just because a girl modelled clothes or worked in a beauty-parlour. No reason why they shouldn't be as integral as women in any other kind of job. But Lucinda Mace seemed quite the wrong sort of girl to make Derek a good wife.

"You *must* warn your half-brother," Vivian had insisted. "You couldn't let him marry such a person in ignorance. She ruined my life, you know."

Tonight in the Savoy, Max stared at Lucinda.

How wrong one could be in one's summing up of a person at first sight, he thought, grimly. If he hadn't known the truth he would have imagined Derek's fiancée to be pure as the driven snow. She looked so exquisite in her white chiffon dress. He had never seen a more beautiful girl. No wonder young Derry had fallen for her. He could well believe it. And now Lucinda looked up from the menu and gave Max a quick rather timid smile. It should have melted the hardest heart but Max entirely misinterpreted it. After what Vivian had said, he thought it was not a gentle, unspoken appeal that he should like her for Derek's sake, but an attempt to flirt even with *him*, her future brother-in-law. He did not return the smile. He saw her colour and look quickly away.

Derek addressed him:

"I say, Max, how long are you going to be in London? You and Lucinda and I must see a lot of each other."

Max answered the question but ignored the last words.

"I may be in London some time—waiting for my next orders. I may not even go back to Kenya."

"That will be great. You'll be here for our marriage," said Derek with a proud look at his fiancée's bright chestnut head.

Max carefully stubbed his cigarette end on an ashtray.

"Is it to be soon? We're only just celebrating the engagement tonight, aren't we?"

Derek laughed.

"We don't intend to wait too long. We neither of us believe in very long engagements, do we, darling?"

"No," said Lucinda.

No, thought Max, *you want to get married as quickly as you can, my girl, and hook the eager, unsuspecting fish.*

Lucinda chose her dinner then tried to concentrate on some trivial remark that was being made to her by Iris. She felt thoroughly unnerved. She could not bear the way Derry's half-brother was looking at her. There was such a deadly coldness about Max. It didn't tally with all the nice things Derek had said about his 'fine, warm-hearted brother'. She could feel that Max had no warmth for her. And of course she could only take it for granted that he had been told by Vivian Brill-Burrie.

I must speak to Vivian, she decided.

"Darling, you're not concentrating," she heard Iris's laughing voice.

"No," said Lucinda dully.

"Your brother-in-law's a *smasher,*" said Iris, "I've never seen such a marvellous-looking man, have you?"

"No," said Lucinda in the same dull voice.

"Nobody would think those two even had one parent in common—they're so different."

"Yes," said Lucinda.

"*Darling,* what *is* the matter?" Iris asked, suddenly aware that her friend was looking pale and worried and that all her original fresh radiance had vanished.

Suddenly Lucinda got up. She *must* speak to Vivian. She *must.*

"Oh, goodness," she said in a high-pitched voice. "I left my compact in the powder-room. I must go and rescue it."

Quickly she walked away from the party. Derek murmured to Max:

"Isn't she gorgeous? Aren't I a lucky fellow?"

"M'm yes . . . oh . . . er . . . yes . . ." Max mumbled and lit a fresh cigarette.

Derek embarked on a youthful and enthusiastic list of his fiancée's virtues.

"And her parents are jolly nice people. Mr Mace is a Jobber on the Stock Exchange. He's had rather bad luck. Lucinda has been very good. One of the things I most admire about her is the hard way she's worked and helped her people."

Max mumbled something again. He looked toward the Maces. He found nothing to criticise in either of them. They seemed just ordinary, nice people. He remembered now that Vivian had said they *were* quite nice and that she felt rather sorry for them because they never had been able to control the girl they nicknamed 'Cindy'. Also that Cindy had led them a dance ever since she left school.

When Lucinda had walked away just now he had taken note of her grace and her lovely legs and ankles. Of course she had all the physical allure—all of it! But it disgusted him to think that she had used it even when she was eighteen to wreck the marriage of a woman like Mrs. Brill-Burrie. Added to which Vivian had suggested that there had been other scandals in which Lucinda was involved. Poor old Derry! He had been properly taken in.

"What the hell am I going to do?" Max asked himself. "I can, of course, sit back and do nothing and let him marry her. A lot of people would say I oughtn't to interfere. But if Mrs. Brill-Burrie is to be believed, it would be absolutely wrong of me to let it go on. He should be told, then make up his own mind."

In any case, Vivian had even hinted that she herself would warn Derek rather than see the boy wreck his life. Vivian obviously felt very strongly about the whole situation. Little wonder as she, personally, had been so involved.

Now Lucinda, her heart thumping unpleasantly fast, reached the table at which Vivian Brill-Burrie was sitting. The palms of her hands felt damp with nervousness. She blurted out the hated name.

"*Vivian* . . . hello! . . ."

The well-remembered amber eyes looked up at her with the old cat-like quality which had at first mesmerised Cindy and later filled her with repugnance.

"Hello," Vivian replied in an ice-cold voice, but made no attempt to introduce Lucinda to her escort who had risen to his feet.

"Could I . . . do you mind . . . if I just speak to you a moment?" stammered the younger girl.

"This is hardly the time——" began Vivian.

"I must speak to you," interrupted Lucinda quite desperately, feeling herself quite driven to this unorthodox behaviour. "It's important."

"Oh, very well," said Vivian.

In the powder-room, whilst making pretence at combing their hair, the two spoke in undertones. Lucinda went straight to the point.

"You met my fiancé's brother . . . in Nairobi, didn't you?"

"I did."

"He told you about our engagement?"

"He did."

"And you told him what happened at the Alexandra?"

"Yes."

"Why? Why?" asked Lucinda in a strangled voice. "Why did you want to be so spiteful—so malicious? It's all so long ago. Why did you want to drag it all up?"

Now Vivian's gaze flicked up and down the young graceful figure in the white dinner dress. The old bitter jealousy and dislike revived. She had always been so envious of this girl's youth and beauty. She felt even more so now—two years later.

Nothing had gone right for Vivian. She had chucked Wilfred out of her life. He had eventually sent her the evidence and allowed her to divorce him—sick and tired of her at last. But the man she had wanted hadn't married her in the end. She had done herself no good by getting her freedom.

She was two years older now and although she took the pains to preserve her looks she was rapidly finding that men did not respond quite so sympathetically when she used the old weapons such as her 'migraine' and her 'helplessness'.

It hadn't been all roses out in Nairobi even though she had found admirers there. But when she met Max Chalmerson she was bowled over by him. Once she knew that Lucinda Mace was his future sister-in-law, she resolved to queer Cindy's pitch again. She wasn't going to have Cindy getting in first with *her* story. Vivian meant to see a lot more of Max, and for that reason alone she left her cousin's house in Nairobi and returned to London.

She still had enough money to live on without working and she still intended to find another husband. But it was now her intention that Max Chalmerson should be the one. So she was determined to use every weapon she could think of, no matter how unsporting, to ensure that Lucinda was put in the wrong. She wouldn't allow Max to grow fond of *Cindy*.

"You nearly wrecked my reputation after the affair at Oversands. You behaved abominably to me. Why do you want to hurt me all over again?" Lucinda demanded, her large eyes glittering at Vivian.

Vivian smiled.

"My dear girl. I have only told Max Chalmerson the truth."

"The truth," repeated Lucinda bitterly, "I bet it wasn't! I bet you made it sound far worse than it was—just as you did at The Alexandra."

"If the cap fits, you must wear it," said Vivian.

"But you know it doesn't, and never did."

Vivian rearranged the big pink pearls which she wore around her throat.

"If this is all you want to say to me, you must excuse me," she drawled. "I must get back to my friend."

"Wait," said Lucinda, trembling. "I want to know something. Do you mean to try and come between Derek and me? Do you want to bust up my engagement? Is *that* it?"

"I'm not interested in you, really."

"But you *are*—you must be, or you wouldn't have told Max about me."

Vivian shrugged.

"I thought it my duty to warn him what sort of a girl his brother is going to marry——"

Lucinda gasped.

"How monstrous. You haven't changed. You're the most frightfully evil woman I've ever met in my life."

"*You* are the evil one," said Vivian smoothly. "Don't forget it was through you I lost my husband."

"You know that's a foul lie!" said Lucinda passionately. "And if you go on telling people that I shall get my father to sue you for libel."

Now Vivian gave a tinkle of laughter.

"Oh, my dear, I wouldn't if I were you. Mud sticks, you know. You escaped one court case. If you insist on another, it will make things so *very* ugly for you. Besides, what does it matter what I tell Max? If he passes the news on to his half-brother, it will be up to Derek as to whether he marries you or not. You must be very nervous of losing him."

And with another laugh, Vivian swept on.

Lucinda sat at the dressing-table alone for a moment, staring blindly at herself, trying to recover her composure. She could hardly credit the fact that Vivian's malice could span the years so remorselessly. What an atrocious stroke of luck for *her*, Lucinda, that Vivian should have met Max. As for those last words about being 'nervous of losing Derek', Lucinda could only hope that if Derek heard, he loved her enough to believe *her* side of the story.

But would he? Hadn't she always been terrified that Derek might get to hear about the past and think the worst?

Oh, God! thought Lucinda, *What an engagement party!*

Somehow she knew she must pull herself together and go back to her table.

6

MRS. MACE was surprised when, in the middle of getting breakfast on that Sunday morning, Cindy in her dressing-gown walked into the kitchen.

"Why, darling, I thought you'd be sleeping late after last night. We weren't home till two and——"

"I couldn't sleep," interrupted Lucinda, and added abruptly, "Too much rich food, I expect."

"I've just got a cup of tea for Daddy. Pour yourself out one, dear. The party was a great success, wasn't it?"

"Yes," said Lucinda, avoiding her mother's smiling gaze.

As she carried the tea-tray toward the door, the mother glanced at Lucinda over her shoulder. She felt some surprise. What was wrong with the child? She looked terribly pale. At her age she ought to be able to stand up to one late night.

"Have you got a headache——?" she began but once again was interrupted.

"I'm all right, Mummy. Just a headache, as you say."

"I thought it a lovely party," sighed Mrs. Mace. "God-mama was in great form, wasn't she? And you looked so *beautiful*. We all thought so. And *what* a handsome man you've got for a future brother-in-law! Daddy said he was most intelligent. They talked a lot."

With this, Mrs. Mace vanished. Lucinda poured out her tea and stirred it mechanically. A headache! It was more than that, she thought. She had a feeling of sick despair. She had only slept in snatches and been awake since six o'clock brooding, although she wouldn't tell Mummy that.

As she sipped the hot tea she caught sight of her face in a little mirror that hung in the kitchen. She thought that she looked forty instead of half that age. Just *awful*. She'd been so tired and upset last night, she hadn't bothered to remove her make-up. The mascara on her lashes had run and made her look hollow-eyed. Her lips were smudged. She shut her eyes as though the light hurt them. It was a glorious morning —quite the best they'd had this August so far, and she was supposed to be driving with Derek—*and* Max—down to the river for lunch. Derek had made the suggestion. They were going to pick her up just before noon.

"I won't ring you up and disturb you, my angel," Derek had said when he kissed her good-night. "Sleep late and relax. You're looking a bit tired."

Her looks betrayed her, she thought, both to her mother and her fiancé. But neither could know of the appalling fears that had made a stricken thing of her ever since she had seen and spoken to Vivian Brill-Burrie at the Savoy.

"Oh, God," she had kept thinking, "*Oh, God*, what's going to happen now?"

The party that was in Derek's and her honour had turned out to be a fiasco so far as she was concerned. The others had all enjoyed themselves. They had laughed and talked and danced and it had been a splendid dinner. How she had envied Iris who had seemed blissful with her latest boy friend to whom she was probably going to get engaged. A charming boy named Christopher Lowe—studying medicine at Guy's. Lucinda had danced with him. She had danced with her father, too. He seemed to have shaken off the cares of the City and thoroughly enjoyed the celebration. And of course she had danced nearly all the time with Derek, only once with Max. Politely he had issued the one invitation and politely she had accepted. But they had not repeated the dance. He was in fact a far better dancer than his brother. In normal circumstances she would have enjoyed it. But he had been so cold, so formal that he had frozen her. He had avoided making any personal reference to Derek or their approaching marriage. Either he had talked about Kenya and the present political situation which he called 'tricky', or the troubles in Europe— or Russia's latest rocket-triumph. She had longed to blurt out a few leading questions and satisfy herself as to what Max really knew or felt about her. Find out if he had been told a lot of dastardly lies by Vivian, and it he intended to pass them on to Derek. But he had never given her the opportunity. She had found herself dancing with him like an automaton—a puppet whose strings he was pulling, making her do and say things against her will. All the time she had grown more and more conscious of Max's extraordinary strength of will—his dominant personality—the tremendous difference between his quiet, young brother and himself. Max had a quality that over-awed Lucinda and yet excited her admiration. Derek had said he was unique. Now she could believe it. But Max held her while they danced as lightly and casually as he would have done a complete stranger. Only once had he looked down into her eyes—that was when he thanked her in that terrifyingly polite voice for dancing with him.

She had sat down feeling herself tremble. Those grey, black-lashed eyes of his were so very penetrating—she was sure they could see right through her.

"I hope they do," she had thought hysterically. "I hope he sees into my mind and heart and *knows* that I'm *not* what Vivian says I am."

If only she could be sure what he was going to *do*. The suspense was killing. At one moment she almost decided to go to Derek this morning, herself, and tell him everything. She had never been a coward. She had always despised people who shirked unpleasant truths. But somehow this was different. It was very complicated. She knew only too well how black things had looked against her at the actual time of the Brill-Burrie scandal.

Perhaps, she thought feverishly while she drank her tea, I'll go and talk it over with Aunt Mary. I'll make some excuse not to go down to the river with the boys. I'll get Mummy to tell them I'm ill . . .

But if she did that, she supposed Derek would rush round and insist on seeing her. Whatever she did there would be trouble. She thought of Derek's good-night kiss—the tender way he had laid his cheek against hers and murmured against her hair:

"This has been a marvellous night, sweetheart. I'm so terribly proud of you and I'm sure Max adores you, too. I could see how you impressed him."

Poor, fond, deluded Derek, she thought. If only he knew what his half-brother *really* felt about her.

If only she knew it herself!

She began to pace up and down the kitchen—hot and restless. The glorious sunlight outside seemed a mockery. It would have been such a wonderful day on the river with Derek and Max . . . if only Vivian hadn't appeared on the scene and wrecked everything!

Last night's conversation with Vivian had shown Lucinda one thing definitely—that she need expect neither truth nor mercy from that quarter. It would be futile even to try and appeal to Vivian again.

Almost she nerved herself to go along to Derek's flat and pour out the whole story to him. It would of course be awful to see him change from the happy, blissful young man he had been last night, into a man suddenly poisoned by suspicion. He believed in her so implicitly now. *Would he* accept her story of what had happened at the Alexandra Hotel two years ago? Wouldn't it be just *her* word against Mrs. Brill-Burrie's? And of course Vivian would draw in a number of her old Putney cronies and admirers to put in *their* spoke. Quite a few might be prepared to remember that she, Cindy, had once had a reputation for being rather a 'naughty girl'—quite apart from the Brill-Burrie affair.

"I must do something," Lucinda said to herself, "or I shall go mad."

Then she reversed her decision. No—she wouldn't go to Derek now. She would talk to Max. While her parents were drinking their tea together safely up in their bedroom, where they couldn't overhear, Lucinda went into her father's little

study and telephoned Max's hotel. He was staying at the
Royal Court in Sloane Square.

When he answered the phone, the sound of his voice had the
same effect upon Lucinda as it had done last night. An in-
explicable effect. His was a clear, direct voice. He had rather
an abrupt manner of speaking. It undermined her courage
in some curious way. She felt that if she was in a witness box
and had just been addressed by a brilliant barrister, she could
not have felt weaker—or more intimidated.

She stammered:

"I . . . I must see you."

"I understand we're all going down to Bray at midday——"
he began, coolly.

"I must see you before then," she interrupted.

"Does Derek know?"

"No."

"Then don't you think we had better wait till we all three
meet?"

"No," Lucinda persisted in a breathless, even frenzied
voice. "I must see you alone, first."

A moment's pause and then from Max:

"Very well, as you wish."

She didn't wish it at all, but the situation was being forced
upon her. She wished with all her heart that everything was
as she had once hoped it would be and that she could feel that
this big, handsome, powerful man was going to be *her* brother
as well as Derek's. But the brother-and-sister association between Max and herself was right out of it. He obviously had
no wish to be either affectionate or friendly. Vivian must have
done her work very thoroughly.

Fragments of remarks that Derek had made during the
evening flitted through Lucinda's agitated brain.

*Max will love you . . . you will love him . . . he'll admire
everything about you, as I do. He'll be so glad I've found the
perfect girl . . . Max knows how hard I am to please . . . he will
appreciate what a pearl my darling Cindy is. . . .*

Derek didn't often call her by that nickname, 'Cindy', and she didn't really like it any more. It reminded her too much of the old frivolous days when boys like Tommy Marchent had teased her with the popular song:

'*Cindy, oh, Cindy . . .*'

First of all in fun . . . afterwards in mockery . . . *after she had got herself into such a mess.*

"Lucinda is a beautiful name," Derek had once said to her. "I've looked it up and I see that it's a seventeenth-century poet's variation of Lucy, and that it was derived from *St. Lucia* who was a martyr under one of the Roman emperors. A popular saint in the middle ages. *You* are my saint and very popular with me . . ." he had ended, laughing, caressing her hair. She had been conscious of his passionate love for her and his deep admiration which had always scared her because of its idealistic quality.

'*St. Lucia the martyr,*' she thought now on this particular Sunday morning, and laughed aloud with the irony of it. She said:

"I'll come straight round to your hotel, Max."

She made an excuse to her parents that she wanted to run round the corner to see Iris for an hour.

She dressed in a hurry and didn't bother with her make-up. When she arrived at Max's hotel she was deadly pale. She had tied her long chestnut hair back into a pony-tail which she did not often do. It made her look very young. Max Chalmerson confessed himself a little shaken to see how youthful she was in her candy-striped dress, her short white jacket, and with that tied-back hair. Younger and somehow more appealing than the sophisticated model-girl of last night in her chiffon evening dress.

Looking down into her eyes he could see that she was scared and worried. But he thought:

'*This is one of her gambits—this Little-Girl-Lost expression. I'm quite sure she knows what she's doing. She knows all there is to know about attracting men and she's going to play the pathetic child with me. Perhaps this is what got old Derek in the first place—quite apart from her amazing good looks. Well, I'm on my guard!'*

Yes, he had spoken to Vivian over the phone already this morning. She had rung him from her sister's flat where she was staying.

"I feel so strongly about this, Max—you *must* warn your poor young brother," she kept saying, "and don't be taken in by her yourself if she puts over the sob-stuff. That's how she got my husband. He fell for that 'nobody-understands-me' act."

"Would you like some coffee?" Max asked Lucinda as they walked across the lounge and sat down at a secluded table by the window.

"No, thank you. And please do stop being so . . . so formal with me . . . so *horribly* polite," Lucinda suddenly blurted out.

Max raised his brow.

"I'm sorry if my attitude displeases you."

"You don't intend it to be *pleasing*, do you?" she asked resentfully.

"My dear girl——" he began.

"Oh, *stop it*!" broke in Lucinda with passion now, and a bright flush on each cheek. "Please don't cover up any more. Tell me what you're thinking—what you're really thinking about me."

Max spread his long legs in front of him, crossed his ankles and lit a cigarette.

Miserable though Lucinda was, she noted the strange grace of this big man's gestures. How utterly divorced he was from her concept of what a brother of Derek's would be like. They were utterly different. A woman would scarcely feel tenderly about Max Chalmerson. She would either love him to distraction—or hate him. And for the moment Lucinda hated Max.

He offered her a cigarette. She took one and smoked nervously. Then he said:

"Right. Let's put an end to the skirmishing and join battle. To begin with, I suppose you'll admit you fascinated my brother into this engagement."

"That isn't a very attractive way of putting it."

"How would your describe it?" He looked at her through narrowed lids.

She flung back her head.

"Derek and I met and fell in love, that's all."

Max watched her through a curl of cigarette smoke. He saw the lovely line of her long throat and the way her chestnut hair sprang crisply from her smooth brow—and how her long lashes fluttered nervously as she spoke. By God, she would be a temptation to any man, he thought. No wonder old Derek had fallen so flat on his face. What a pity, *what a pity* she wasn't all that she ought to be.

"Okay," he said. "You met and you fell in love and——?"

"And I wasn't gold-digging was I?" went on Lucinda defiantly. "I knew as well as you do that Derek isn't well-off."

"Oh, he won't do so badly later on. There's a Trust from his mother which gives him a small income now, and he'll get the capital when he's thirty."

"But he's not *rich*, so you can't accuse me of being a fortune-hunter."

"Very well, you're not a fortune-hunter. You just want to get married."

"Why not?" she found herself trembling again as she had trembled last night when Max first spoke to her. "Most women need security."

"And you especially. It's something you've always lacked, isn't it?"

The cruelty of this made her gasp a little. But there was a strangely logical side to Lucinda's mind. She could even find an excuse for Max's brutality. He was his brother's guardian and friend. He loved the boy. He was only trying to do his best for *him*. And after all, Vivian had told Max dreadful things about her.

"Listen," said Lucinda, "I know why you're talking to me like this. You don't think I'm good enough for Derek—or put it the other way. You think *he* is too good for *me*."

"Precisely," said Max.

"So you want to try and make him break with me?"

"I think," said Max in a slow, deliberate voice, "that if he doesn't yet know what happened two years ago, you ought to tell him, and if you don't—you're doing him an injustice."

"Do *you* know what happened?"

"I only know what I've been told."

"But you have no proof?"

"Have you," he counter-questioned, "any proof that Mrs. Brill-Burrie's story is a mere fabrication?"

"It may not be altogether a fabrication," said Lucinda, beginning to feel cornered. "I mean . . . there *were* circumstances which may make things look black for me—but if she says I was having an affair with her husband, that's a wicked lie."

"It is precisely what she does say. She also assures me that all your mutual friends who were in the hotel with you on that holiday know that you were found in the doctor's bedroom. Even your own godmother was a witness, apparently."

Lucinda sat forward, her young face white and strained, her eyes blazing.

"Yes, I *was* in Wilfred Brill-Burrie's bedroom. But not . . . not because we were *lovers*."

"Oh, my dear!" said Max. "Surely you're not going to tell me that a young girl of eighteen goes into the bedroom of a married man in a seaside hotel at one or two o'clock in the morning, merely to talk about tennis or croquet."

Lucinda bit her lip until the blood came.

"No—it wasn't to talk about games or . . . or to talk at all. I thought it was somebody else's room. Vivian planned it all. It was a wicked scheme. She wanted to get rid of her husband . . . and I can tell you the whole story——"

"Her version," said Max in his inexorable voice, "doesn't

tally with yours. But it sounds much more probable. It seems that at that time Mrs. Brill-Burrie was quite happily married, only her husband had an eye for young girls and *you* led him on. She says the whole affair led ultimately to a divorce. You were not actually involved in the second case but you were the start of all the trouble. You don't deny that you were found in his bedroom, do you?"

"No, I don't, but I can tell you exactly why I went there," she exclaimed, clenching her hands.

"Fire away," said Max.

"Oh, you *want* to believe the worst of me," she broke out hysterically, "and to take Vivian's word against mine. You seem to *want* to break my heart and Derek's, too."

Now suddenly Max's attitude changed. He looked tense and a little weary. He found the whole thing extremely distasteful. He was even sorry for the girl because she was so young. And perhaps she really was in love with Derek now and wanted to turn over a new leaf. He must not preach tolerance to young Derry and be too intolerant himself, he reflected with some irony.

"Look here, Lucinda," at length he said, "I haven't the slightest wish to break yours or Derek's heart. Derry is my prime concern. He's all I've got in this world—the only one left in my family—and I'm under oath to the man who was the father of us both to look after his interests through thick and thin. I don't intend to break that oath. I am not going to sit down and watch Derek marry a girl whom he believes to be an angel, only to find things out later on when it's too late. That would be a tragedy for one of his nature. I *know* Derek."

"So do I," said Lucinda in a smothered voice, and the tears started to her eyes but she blinked them away in a fierce endeavour not to break down in front of this man. This powerful, ruthless man who seemed to hold her whole life's happiness between his hands.

He went on:

"Then, you'll admit that because he is so high-principled it would do him irreparable harm if he married you, *then* discovered you were not what he had thought you."

Lucinda went scarlet.

"But I'm not what *you* think, either. I may have fooled around when I was younger, and I know there was all that scandal about the Brill-Burries, but I was never guilty of . . . adultery." She gasped out the hateful word.

"Then, my dear, why on earth should Mrs. Brill-Burrie have told me all this?"

"Because she's a spiteful, malicious woman who wanted her freedom and used me as a pawn in order to try and get it."

Max rubbed the back of his head in a puzzled way. Lucinda spoke with such conviction. Yet Vivian, too, had convinced him that her version of this story was a true one.

"Look . . ." he said, "Mrs. Brill-Burrie was older than her husband and never very well—is not that so? She adored him and you played fast-and-loose with the man. She suspected you, and went along to his room and found you in there. Surely that *is* the truth?"

"No, not altogether."

"Very well then," said Max, "let's hear *your* story."

She began to pour it out, but nervousness and distress made her tell it badly. It sounded disjointed. And now, two years later, even absurd. As she told Max how Vivian had suggested that she should act the cat-burglar and climb along the balcony and scare Zoë Ennerman into handing over her jewels, because Zoë was supposed to have that room, she realised how far-fetched it must appear. She kept on denying that she and Wilfred Brill-Burrie had ever been lovers. Wilfred, himself, would tell Max, she said. Where was Wilfred? Nobody knew. There was nobody actually to swear that the two of them had never exchanged a single kiss that night at the Alexandra.

At the end of this outburst, Lucinda said wildly:

"You don't believe one word I've said. Oh, I can see you don't!"

Then Max said in quite a kind voice:

"Frankly, I don't. It's a bit too unrealistic. Besides, for the life of me I can't imagine why poor little Mrs. Brill-Burrie should have trumped up the whole thing."

"You don't understand how wicked she is. She's used bits that *are* true, such as me being in her husband's bedroom— which I was——" began Lucinda, passionately. Then she broke down. She stubbed her cigarette in an ashtray and put her face in her hands.

"Oh, *God!*" she whispered.

Max looked uneasily at the bent lovely head. He was trying hard to rationalise the whole thing. He found himself being caught between the stories of these two women—the young one, and the older. It was not that he was in love with Vivian —he was not even flattered by her obvious *penchant* for him. But he had felt sorry for the frail, big-eyed, lonely woman whose husband had left her, and naturally indignant against the little wretch who had so flagrantly and callously come between husband and wife. And once he knew the culprit was Derek's chosen wife, it concerned Max vitally. Anyhow, Derek ought to be told. On that point Max was adamant. But he was still not particularly pleased with himself about it. Lucinda seemed so utterly miserable. She had not taken up a defiant, callous attitude. Was it only because she didn't like to see her chances of marriage slipping by and so was putting on this 'innocent act'? Or was she sincerely in love with Derry? Max wished that he knew.

This morning over the telephone in her most pathetic voice, Vivian had said to him:

"Beware, my dear Max. I know Cindy only too well. She'll put over the sob-stuff beautifully. That's what she did with my husband and that's why *he* fell for her."

Max lit another cigarette and scowled at the tip of it.

He must harden his heart against pretty Lucinda and think only about young Derek. He just couldn't tolerate the thought of Derry being disillusioned *after* marriage. Perhaps it was unfortunate for Lucinda, but out in Nairobi recently there had been just such another case. A very nice army subaltern had been taken in by a most attractive girl whom everybody knew to be quite unscrupulous where her love affairs were concerned. Another one with big dewy eyes like Lucinda's! And in this case the boy had insisted on marrying her. Then came the reckoning. She had left him for someone else and the boy had taken to drink and been asked to resign his commission. Max knew, of course, that Derek would never take to drink—he was too moderate and sensible a fellow, but it wouldn't do him much good if he woke up too late to the realisation that his young wife was *that* sort of girl.

Why, Max asked himself, do such things have to happen to the good chaps like Derek? If it had been me, I could have coped. *I* can take care of myself. And I dare say if I had the chance I could even knock some sense into Lucinda. I'm sure she has some good stuff in her. One could make something of her.

He spoke to her gently.

"Look, Lucinda," he said, "there's no point in our going on like this. I admit I'm confused between your story and Vivian's. It's getting us nowhere. Only one thing remains clear. My brother adores *and* believes in you. I don't think you ought to get married without telling him about your past. And I rather think that if *you* don't tell him, Mrs. Brill-Burrie will. She's a very high-minded woman and she doesn't think it fair, after what you did to her, that you should deceive Derek. She says it would be marriage under false pretences."

Lucinda looked up at Max with the utmost bitterness.

Vivian a high-minded woman . . . that was one big joke! Oh, how terribly cruel and stubborn this man can be, she thought. Why doesn't he give me a chance? He's been put completely against me by Vivian.

"Do you mean to tell Derek?" she asked, miserably.

"No," he said. "*You* are going to tell him, yourself."

"I?"

"Yes. I'm not going to Bray this morning. I shall leave you two alone. You can talk to him and tell him the truth."

"Then you don't believe that Vivian only involved me in all this beastliness because she wanted her freedom?"

"I think it rather a tall story. But *you* tell Derek all the facts and let *him* decide for himself whether or not he wants to go on with his marriage. If he does, it is no longer any business of mine."

"Very well," said Lucinda.

She gained her feet. Her large, luminous eyes looked up at Max with a brilliance that confounded him because in spite of all the accusations which Vivian Brill-Burrie had levelled against this girl, he had found no weakness or hypocrisy about Lucinda.

And now suddenly it was Max who showed signs of weakness—of doubt. He began:

"Of course, if you think it fair to go through with the wedding and let Derek remain ignorant——"

She interrupted:

"No, I have no intention of doing that now. I'm only sorry I've been a coward and not told him before. But I didn't want to risk losing him. Now, somehow, I don't believe I *will*. I think he'll stand by me. His mind won't have been poisoned by Vivian as yours is, before I've been given a chance to speak. I'm not afraid any more—of you, or the truth. I'll go now—this moment—to Derek's flat and tell him everything."

7

"WAIT——" began Max.

She interrupted again:

"What for? Until *you* can go and see him first and say all sorts of awful things about me?"

The red crept slowly up under his tan.

"I'm not quite such a so-and-so as that, I assure you."

"I don't care what you are—I only know that you're trying to wreck my happiness with Derek, and since you believe every word Vivian Brill-Burrie has said I've got to make sure that Derek *doesn't* believe it."

Max now found himself at a loss for words. There was a quality in this girl that baffled him. Of course she might be behaving in this way out of bravado; realising that she hadn't got away with the 'angel' stuff, she was at bay—on the defensive. She wanted Derek and the security of marriage. He was a nice, good, clean-living Englishman. She wouldn't give him up easily.

He watched her walk away. What a straight back she had. How beautifully she moved. Hadn't Derek said that she did a bit of modelling as well as being a *vendeuse*? She was extraordinarily attractive. And if that fresh charm, that dewy-eyed innocence, masked a cheap little coquette, she certainly possessed all the right weapons. He could see that Derek wouldn't have stood a chance. Why, Max thought cynically, *he* himself might have felt drawn to her—mesmerised was the better word—if Vivian hadn't warned him.

He wondered just how much, or how little, Lucinda would tell Derek. Even while she was walking away from him he began to doubt the wisdom of his first move. *Ought* he to have interfered? It was a debatable point. He was quite sure some people would have told him bluntly to mind his own business.

But Derek *was* his business, he argued. He was a simple, trusting sort of fellow with no experience of women. How could he let such a boy go through with marriage, believing implicitly in his fiancée, when she had come between a husband and wife two years ago. She had almost been cited in a divorce case. Vivian had left no room for doubt in Max's mind that young 'Cindy' as they used to call her had not visited her husband's bedroom for the most innocent of reasons. As for that story about pretending to be a jewel-burglar, it was a lot of nonsense. No—he mustn't start regretting that he had put a spoke in the wheel. Let Lucinda come into the open with Derek and then what Derek chose to do about it, was his own affair. Max could feel that he had at least tried to save him.

Max had promised to take Vivian to dinner that night at Claridges. Out in Nairobi he had been impressed by little Mrs. Brill-Burrie's dark, striking good looks and mature charm. She was a witty companion and he had dated her a number of times. They had dined and danced together and struck up the sort of gay, amusing friendship in which a man can only too easily become embroiled out in Kenya. The climate, the exotic vegetation, the glamorous nights all contributed to that sort of thing, and Max had just come back from a long tour of the 'wilds', so attractive feminine company was welcome. All the more so because Max had a soft side to him. Basically he was neither as hard nor as ruthless as he appeared. Vivian had appealed to him because she seemed lonely and still badly shaken up by the loss of her husband. These terrible 'migraines' from which she suffered now and again also made her an object for his pity. A woman who had suffered and was still suffering, mentally and physically, was far more likely to receive attention from Max than the type whom he so often encountered in Nairobi. The hard-drinking, hard-riding, hard-swearing kind of girl who crouched on cocktail stools in the bars of all the smart hotels, 'soaking gin'. The gold-diggers and the husband-hunters—the kind Max always avoided. He had, of course, made sure that his friendship with Vivian was a casual one. It was only now when he was back in England, that he wondered whether it wasn't a little foolish of him to go on seeing her. He had no intention of being caught in marriage by Vivian, or indeed by any other woman. And, curiously enough, after last night (and again after this morning's encounter with Lucinda) he almost wished he had never met Vivian at all; never had that ugly story about her divorce planted on him.

"Damn!" he said under his breath as he walked out of the hotel into Sloane Square.

He felt restless; even after a long smart walk through the park, unable to settle down to looking up old friends or attending to his overdue correspondence. He could not get Lucinda out of his mind. He found himself burning with curiosity to know how his young half-brother would take it when he heard what Lucinda had to say.

She had some courage, that girl—she might have appealed to him, Max, more strenuously not 'to give her away'; she might have refused to tell Derek a thing. Yes—he had to grant it that Lucinda showed real spirit, the way she had marched off relying on Derek to stand by her. Max even found himself (rather to his own astonishment) hoping that the boy *would* believe in her.

Meanwhile, Lucinda knowing that she faced the most important crisis of her life, hailed a taxi and drove to Derek's flat in Lexham Gardens.

She had been there only once before and, as she told herself bitterly, in much happier circumstances; soon after they had first declared their love for each other. He had taken her home one afternoon to look through some old albums of photographs; of himself as a boy, and afterwards at school and the 'varsity. There had been a few photographs of his parents, too, that he wanted his future wife to see. She remembered what a happy afternoon it had been. She had made tea for him afterwards and they had sat together on the sofa in the small sitting-room. The flat was a small one at the top of one of those big converted houses.

They had been so much in love. But she had noted at the time how restrained he was in his lovemaking even after they were officially engaged. At times, when passion quickened his pulses, they used to kiss with all the fervour of their newly discovered delight, then he would draw away. His blue eyes shining at her, he would stroke her hair and murmur:

"I mustn't let you go completely to my head. You are too attractive, Lucinda."

Although they were utterly alone, he had refrained from kissing her again quite so passionately. He lit a pipe and smoked it and told her stories of his youth, always including tales of Max; his marvellous brother.

I hate Max. I *hate him*, Lucinda told herself violently as she ran up the stairs to Derek's flat.

She longed to tell Max to go back to Kenya and leave her alone. She would never, *never* accept him as a brother-in-law with any affection now. She would always feel that he had tried to harm her, and to make Derry unhappy, too. Yet once she stood outside Derek's front door, she paused. Her passionate resentments, her torrential emotions, seemed to simmer down, down into a positive well of sick fear. *Oh, God,* she thought, *what would she do if Derry didn't believe her? And if he, too, thought her guilty of separating Vivian from her husband?*

Almost she turned and ran away. But she had never been a coward. She resisted that impulse. She rang the bell, white and tense and not at all sure of herself any longer. Derek opened the door.

He was in his shirt-sleeves. His fair hair was ruffled. He seemed to be in the middle of dressing.

He looked at her first with astonishment then delight.

"Lucinda! My angel! What a wonderful surprise. I was coming to fetch *you*."

"Can I come in?"

"But of course, honey. Sorry I'm improperly dressed. I've just dashed back from the garage where I've been washing and polishing *Mr. Moses*."

Normally, this would have brought a gay, amused reply from Lucinda who always took an interest in the old veteran car and maintained that once she was 'Mrs. Moses' she, herself, would help with the polishing. Today there was no smile on her face as she walked into the sitting-room.

"Guy's away for the week-end, isn't he?" she asked.

"Yes."

Guy was the friend who shared Derek's flat—a rather serious, bespectacled young man whom Cindy felt she would never get to know very well, because he had the typical one-track mind of the scientist. He also obviously resented her arrival on the scene, as it meant he must find somebody to take Derek's place in this flat, or move out himself.

When she had first come up here with Derek she had thought how dull and cheerless the sitting-room was—a real bachelor establishment. Not a flower. Ordinary curtains and covers. Dusty piles of books, files and newspapers. No feminine touch. Derek had said he longed for his own home which *she* would decorate and furnish. He, himself, had no particular fads and fancies but great faith in Lucinda's taste. He would leave it all to her.

Now they faced each other, Derek still chatting gaily, unaware that anything was wrong with his fiancée until suddenly he noticed her silence and the strained look on her face. He bent to kiss her and she drew back. He stared at her.

"What's wrong with you? Why no kiss?"

"Because I must talk to you, first."

"But of course, darling. Come and sit down. Have a cigarette."

She accepted the cigarette gratefully. It soothed her nerves. Derek could see her fingers trembling. His own healthy good humour took a downward curve. Her tense condition communicated itself to him.

"Lucinda, nothing wrong at home, I hope?"

"No."

"Then tell me—don't keep me in suspense."

She moistened her lips with the tip of her tongue, for they felt dry—like her throat. She was aware now that she was positively terrified. She even found herself wishing that Derek was an older man—someone upon whose shoulder she could lean while she told her story and be certain of understanding and comfort. Derek *was* rather 'correct' and he *had* idealised her; which made it all the harder to tell him the facts. Even though Vivian had grossly exaggerated the whole affair and given Max a wrong impression, the young Cindy had not been *quite* the serious-minded, sensible girl she was today.

"I don't know how to begin," she said in a low voice.

"Darling, you're putting the wind up me. What in the name of fortune has happened?"

"Nothing immediate. It all happened a long time ago."

"But *what*?"

"I've just been to see Max," she blurted out.

"Brother Max? You've been to see *him*? But why?" Derek's eyes widened in astonishment.

"Because he's been told something about me and he was going to tell *you* but I thought I'd rather do so, myself."

Derek shook his head with a laugh.

"I'm still in the dark."

"I'll try to tell you," she said.

And now Derek heard about Vivian Brill-Burrie and her ex-husband and that whole episode that had taken place down at Oversands two years ago. It all came out about the woman in red whom Max had pointed out to them at the Savoy, last night. The part Lucinda had played in her life. Her warning to Max. It all tumbled out, Lucinda speaking quickly, breathlessly. A Lucinda whom Derek did not recognise. She had always seemed so poised, so reserved. He could not believe that she had ever been an outrageous flirt. But all the time he listened, without stopping her or asking any questions, he became aware of a definite sinking of the heart. A most unpleasant feeling. It was as though a bomb had exploded in his peaceful little flat and shattered that peace for ever.

Lucinda finished on a desperate note.

"You've got to believe that I never did have any sort of an affair with Dr. Brill-Burrie. The sort Vivian told Max I had had. I didn't know even that it was Wilfred's bedroom. I swear I didn't. I thought Zoë was still there. And I swear, too, that I climbed along that balcony from my own room only meaning to get back on Zoë because she'd been so horrible to that young newly married girl who couldn't afford real jewellery. You've *got* to believe me, and not Mrs. Brill-Burrie, please, Derek."

"Just a minute," he said slowly, "I'm afraid I'm a bit confused."

"I don't wonder."

"I'd like to get this a bit straight," he went on. "*Was* there a divorce between the Brill-Burries?"

"Yes, later, but not through me."

"But if Mrs. Brill-Burrie didn't suspect you of having had an affair with her husband, why should she have gone to his room at one in the morning obviously expecting to find you there?"

Lucinda sat in stunned silence. So stunned was she, indeed, by this rather cold searching enquiry, that she felt positively stupid. Incapable of answering. It wasn't at all how Derek should have acted. He should have said at once: '*I believe every word you say.*' But here he was cross-questioning her— being analytical, coldly logical (like all men with scientific minds). It appalled her.

"I just want to know," he continued, "the precise facts. You say that Max was warned by Mrs. Brill-Burrie that you had played fast-and-loose with her husband, and that there was a frightful scandal at the time because you were found in his bedroom."

She nodded.

"It is true that I was found in there and that there *was* a scandal, but——"

"So what Mrs. Brill-Burrie told my brother had *some* truth in it?" he interrupted.

"*Some* truth, yes, but nothing like all of it."

"I see. And Max meant to warn me?"

"Yes, he thought you ought to know about it before you married me."

"I see," said Derek again.

He got up and walked across the room. He looked out. The sky was clouding over. It wasn't going to be so fine after all. Everything had clouded—in a big way, he thought. This was the biggest shock he'd ever received. Then on an impulse he swung round and exclaimed:

"I *can't* believe it, Lucinda."

"What can't you believe?" she demanded, her hopes rising, and the light coming back into her large, frightened eyes.

"That you could ever have acted in such a way. Why, you were only eighteen or nineteen at the most. It doesn't make sense. You're not *like* that."

"But I've always told you that you put me on too high a pedestal, Derek darling," she said slowly. "In fact, you scared me because right from the start you declared I was a sort of angel with wings. I agree that for the last couple of years I haven't looked to the right or left of me. But I *was* a flirt in the old days. I can't deny it. I tried to tell you so once and you just shut me up."

He flushed.

"It never struck me that you'd been involved in a . . . a public scandal."

Again she felt stunned. She said:

"I was very young and stupid at the time. But I'm honestly glad you know now. I've always felt rather guilty because I never told you. But everybody advised me not to because it was so long ago and not all that important."

"I think it *was* important," he said, frowning. "So important anyhow that a woman meets my brother in Nairobi and tells him about it and Max thinks it important I should also be told."

"But, Derek, I repeat what I've said before—Vivian grossly exaggerated the whole episode. Please believe that."

Now he looked at her beautiful, sorrowful face and felt bitterly disappointed because Max must now think badly of her. He had so wanted Max to admire her.

Derek was the type who must always look up to the person he loved, just as he looked up to Max, and had done to his own mother when she was alive. He could not really love somebody he did not respect. Of course, he reflected, there might be less in this story than appeared on the surface but why should Mrs. Brill-Burrie have told such a tale if it was all lies? He could not thank her for her interference but he could quite understand Max not wanting him to marry any girl who was sailing under false pretences. Lucinda hadn't breathed a word of it. She had, in fact, deceived him, he thought with sudden resentment.

He said:

"I wish to God you'd told me this of your own accord."

Then Lucinda froze.

"Does that mean you might not have proposed to me if you had known?" she asked.

He coloured and avoided her gaze.

"I don't say that. I'm sure I'd have proposed. But I think it was odd, darling, that you kept so quiet about it."

"Not at all. I thought the whole thing was over and done with. I've never asked *you* searching questions about your past. I didn't expect you to pry into mine."

He floundered:

"Look here . . . I say . . . I don't think we should have had any secrets from each other. I mean, I have none from you."

"All right. So I've shattered your illusions. Now what are you going to do about it?"

"I say . . ." began Derek again, "look here . . ."

"Well?" she broke in, clenching her hands. "Don't you want me any more now you know that I am the victim of a beastly trumped-up scandal, started by a jealous woman who wanted to get free from her husband?"

"Well, of course, if that's all it was, there's nothing much to it, I suppose," stammered Derek.

She felt suddenly furiously angry with him.

"But you doubt me? You're not a hundred-per-cent sure that my version of the story is the correct one? You're half inclined to believe that Vivian was justified in damning my character after Max first told her we'd got engaged?"

"I didn't say that."

"But you inferred it," interrupted Lucinda. Her eyes blazed now. Her whole body was trembling. And then her voice broke and she put the back of her hand against her quivering lips. She was so desperately disappointed because he had not taken her in his arms and told her that he loved her and would go on loving her and that nothing else mattered, nothing, nothing, *nothing*. If he had suddenly confessed that *he* had been involved in a terrible scandal in his youth and asked her to believe in him, she would have done so—taken his word against anybody else's. What was love worth if not founded on faith?

Now suddenly Derek changed his tune. Passion flared. He pulled her into his arms. He kissed her with a rough sensuality he had never shown her before; in a manner he had never before kissed her. She tore herself away, scarlet, eyes magnified by angry tears.

"Why did you do that?"

"Because I love you."

"Then you're showing your love in quite a new sort of way."

"But I do love you," he stammered. "And I'm still going to marry you. I don't care what this woman says or even what Max thinks."

"Did you kiss me like that just now because you really *love* me or because I'm physically attractive to you?" she asked.

He squirmed.

"Aren't you being rather unpleasant, Lucinda?"

"We aren't having a very pleasant conversation. Look here, Derek, let's face facts. There was once a scandal in which I was involved although I was innocent. A lot of people *did* believe that Wilfred was my boy friend because of the circumstances in which I was found. I dare say Mrs. Brill-Burrie could cook up quite a few more lies and find quite a few people we both knew at the time who would back her up. But there are also people like my own godmother, who was there, who would tell you that I wasn't at *all* in love with Wilfred. *Do* you believe I was innocent, or *don't* you?"

He did not come back with the immediate: '*Yes, of course*', that she hoped for. He hesitated. It was a fatal hesitation—from Lucinda's point of view. It was as though he put a knife straight through her heart. She said under her breath:

"So you still have doubts. You are not quite sure whether I played that prank as a silly school-girl or whether Mrs. Brill-Burrie's accusations are founded on fact?"

Then Derek said:

"Oh, what the hell does it all matter now! As you say, it was long ago. I'm quite ready to forget it."

"Oh, are you?" She gave a long look at his flushed face. "And you're quite ready to forgive me?"

"Yes."

"And to kiss me again as you did just now, whilst all the time you're wondering just how far I went with Wilfred Brill-Burrie?"

"Oh, look here, Lucinda, really——!"

"Well," she broke in wildly, "is it, or isn't it true? Can you tell me definitely, looking me in the eye, that you don't believe one single word Vivian has told your brother?"

He avoided the direct question.

"Darling, do come and sit down—I mean—we're going to be married——"

"We're not," she broke in, and her trembling had become violent. Her face was ashen. She took off her engagement ring and threw it at him. He put out a hand to catch it but missed and it rolled on to the carpet. He stooped to pick it up.

"You're being rather melodramatic, darling. *Really*——"

"No, I'm just breaking our engagement."

"Well I must say that's a bit 'off'. If anybody should break the engagement, it should be me."

She laughed—her eyes hard and unhappy.

"Because of your suspicions!"

"Why are you going on like this? You're being very difficult. I don't understand you."

"No. You don't. Let me explain. We were once in love with each other and we were going to get married. Whatever we've heard about each other shouldn't have mattered—not if we were *really* in love. Max thought the worst of me. You are no better than he is. So do you think I still want to marry you—you, acting the big hero, willing to forgive what the erring little teenager did in a moment of madness? Do you think I want to be your wife knowing that you'll always wonder just how far I was responsible for the Brill-Burrie divorce?"

Now suddenly he felt really afraid; afraid of losing her. He said:

"Cindy, don't let's go on like this. It's too frightful."

"For me it's frightful, because you suspect me."

"I don't see what you've got to complain about," he hedged. "I've told you I still love you and want to marry you."

"Yes, *in spite of* that story. You aren't convinced that I was innocent and that Vivian's abominable accusation was fabricated."

"I . . . I don't really know anything about it. I'm too confused . . ." began Derek, and added: "Darling, do put this ring back on your finger and let's stop fighting."

She drew back from him, shaking her head.

"Thank you—no. Our engagement's over. I couldn't possibly marry a man who could suspect me of carrying on with a married man. You must find somebody else, Derek—a girl who is *quite* above suspicion. I don't want ever to see you or your brother again. You're both smug, pompous prigs— both of you. You don't know what love is——"

Her voice trailed away on a sob. Turning, she ran out of the room and out of the flat, and slammed the door behind her.

8

MAX was a worried man. The more he thought about Lucinda
and his brother, the more doubtful he became as to whether
or not he had done the right thing in forcing the issue between
them. He decided to go straight round to Derek's flat, hoping
that Lucinda would still be there. He would talk to them
both.

He took a taxi to Lexham Gardens, grimacing somewhat
at the trend of his own thoughts. Why he had ever done this,
he didn't now know. He had allowed Vivian to have too much
influence over him. Perhaps the woman *had* exaggerated.
Perhaps he had been much too hasty to condemn. Unconsciously he echoed Lucinda's own words.

"I've been a pompous prig. Why the hell——?"

He was still more worried when he found neither his brother
nor Lucinda at the flat. It seemed deserted. Possibly there
had been some sort of 'bust-up' and they had both gone out,
he reflected. Poor old Derry! No doubt he'd had an unpleasant shock. As for the girl—time and again Max remembered the haunting misery in Lucinda's eyes and reproached
himself for being the cause of it. He should have left things
alone. Of course Derry might have just gone out—might even
be on his way to Sloane Square right now. They could have
crossed each other *en route*. Perhaps they were both on the
way to tell him that they'd had it all out and it was over and the
wedding was still on. Or Lucinda might have taken fright and
not gone round to Derek at all.

Gloomily, Max walked away from his brother's flat. He
would get a taxi in the Cromwell Road. He would go to see
Lucinda. It might be crazy but he was truly sorry now that
he had been intolerant enough to hold the girl's past against
her. He had let his enthusiastic desire to guide young Derry's

footsteps carry him too fast. Anyhow, he must see Lucinda again and have another talk with her.

He then remembered that he didn't know where the Maces lived. He returned to the Royal Court Hotel again and was surprised to find no Derek, and no message. It was long past the time now when the three of them had planned to meet and drive down to the river. Why hadn't Derek contacted him, he wondered.

Max then telephoned the flat owned by Vivian's sister and which Vivian had temporarily taken. When she answered he was curiously annoyed by the creamy smoothness of her voice.

"Why, Max, how *lovely* to hear you . . ."

"I wonder," he said, "if you can give me Lucinda's home address."

There was silence. Max could have sworn that there was somebody else in the room with Vivian. She had put her hand over the microphone. Then she spoke to him again.

"I think you'd better have a word with your brother."

"Is Derek there!" exclaimed Max, astonished.

"Yes, poor darling. Lucky we met and talked for a few minutes when we were both going to find our cars at the Savoy last night. I gave him my address and suggested that he should come and have a drink some time. I rather felt I might be useful to him. He's had a most unhappy scene with Lucinda, and he came straight round to talk to me because he wanted to hear the truth right from the horse's mouth, so to speak. He's very upset, Max, and I don't wonder!"

"Ask him to speak to me," said Max.

"Won't you join us——?" began Vivian.

"Ask him to speak to me," repeated Max, curtly.

Then:

"Hello," said Derek.

"Look here, Derry, I don't know what's happened between you and Lucinda," said Max, "but I want to see you alone if you'd come over to my hotel."

Derek seemed to hesitate.

"No, I'm not coming to Vivian's place," Max forestalled the invitation that he knew his brother was about to make.

Less than a quarter of an hour later, the two brothers faced each other in Max's hotel bedroom. Max was slightly shocked by Derek's appearance. He looked what Max would have described as 'pretty grim'. All the healthy colour and the brightness of his eyes which Max had been pleased to see yesterday, had gone. His mouth was sulky.

"Well," said Max, "out with it. What happened between you and Lucinda?"

"Just what you hoped for, I suppose," said Derek sullenly. "She came and told me about . . . her past. I offered to forgive her and carry on with our marriage but she gave me back the ring and walked out."

Max lit a cigarette. He scowled at the glowing end of it. *What he had hoped for?* Was that altogether true?

"What exactly did Lucinda tell you?" he asked.

"What you already know, except that she denied having ever had the affair, and repeated that silly story about pretending to be a cat-burglar. It seemed to me childish and improbable when she first told it, and now that I've seen Mrs. Brill-Burrie I'm convinced she was lying."

"I see. And what did Vivian say to convince you so thoroughly?"

Derek shrugged his shoulders.

"She told me the whole story—how this husband of hers, this osteopath she calls Wilfred, fell for Lucinda's teenage charm. And how Mrs. Brill-Burrie went along to her husband's bedroom and found Lucinda there. Oh, I don't know, Max—but it speaks for itself. Especially as Mrs. Brill-Burrie assures me she can bring any number of Putney people to witness the fact that Lucinda had a pretty hot reputation in those days."

Max chewed at his lower lip. He felt most uncomfortable; strangely guilty of having brought this avalanche about his brother's ears. On the other hand, it would seem that even if he had not warned Derek, Vivian Brill-Burrie would have done so. '*Hell hath no fury like a woman scorned.*' Wasn't that the saying? Vivian had been rejected in favour of a younger, more attractive girl, and this was her method of revenge. Now that he had had a bit of time to think things over, Max didn't much like Vivian, and he positively hated himself. Suddenly he spoke harshly to his half-brother.

"Damn it, man, if you'd really cared about the girl couldn't you have considered the possibility that the whole episode *was* just childish nonsense and believe her when she said she didn't actually have an affair in the fullest sense with Brill-Burrie?"

"I hoped at first that might be so but I'm quite convinced now, after what Mrs. Brill-Burrie says, that there *was* something in it."

"Lucinda wasn't named in the divorce."

"No, Mrs. Brill-Burrie said they needed a bit more evidence but her husband, himself, owned up to it and then cleared off and finally sent irrefutable evidence of another infidelity so that Mrs. Brill-Burrie could get her freedom."

"I see," said Max, and added, curtly, "and I'm sorry."

"I can't think why," said Derek with a resentful look. "You told Lucinda to tell me everything, didn't you?"

"At the time I thought it was right you should know. You idealised her so blindly."

"Oh, I'm grateful to you," said Derek with a short laugh. "I can't say I'm very happy but I certainly would have felt the whole thing a good deal more if I'd found out about it only after she was my wife."

"So you don't hold it against me that I acted the way I did?" Max asked curiously.

"On the contrary, I'm grateful. I realise that I could never really have respected her, and I think a man's got to be able to respect his wife. Besides, Mrs. Brill-Burrie assured me that I'm well out of it. For your sake as well as mine. She's rather fond of you, you know, Max."

"I couldn't care less," said Max between his teeth.

Now he walked to the window and stared down at the fountain splashing gently in the centre of the square. A man sat near by selling Sunday papers. Out in Kenya on safari Max had sometimes thought how pleasant it would be to get back to London and laze on a Sunday morning, smoking, reading all the 'Sunday Sensations' as he called them. He had flown home full of good cheer—the wish to see young Derek again, and to be present at his wedding. God, he thought, how wrong things had gone! What a mess up! And if the girl was guilty, how plausibly she had maintained her innocence. He still could not stop remembering that wounded look in her large and rather lovely eyes.

"I'm round the bend," he told himself savagely. "Vivian Brill-Burrie and I have torn this thing apart. She's had her revenge and here I am, wishing it hadn't happened."

Then Derek annoyed him by saying in a somewhat pompous manner:

"You must admit, Max, that what I've just said is true. Above all things a fellow must respect his wife. It's a terrible thing to have happened and I've lost someone I adored. But I couldn't have gone on adoring her."

"Couldn't you?" Max asked suddenly, sarcastically.

Derek stared.

"What do you mean?"

"I mean that you might conceivably have taken her word against Mrs. Brill-Burrie's."

"Don't be ridiculous," said Derek, and now he looked at his half-brother in genuine amazement. "How can you possibly argue that way? Mrs. Brill-Burrie swears——"

"Mrs. Brill-Burrie considers that she was hurt by Lucinda and perhaps there *was* some sort of episode, but it may not have been quite so serious. Anyhow, I can tell now that you never really loved Lucinda. If you had, you wouldn't have let her give you back that ring."

Derek exploded.

"Good God! *You* to talk like that. Why, it was you who——"

"I who sounded the warning, yes," Max finished for him. "Sure, I did. And that was as far as I felt my duty lay. But funnily enough, I'd have been quite pleased if you'd come to me and said 'I don't care. I believe in her and always will.' "

"Is that what you wanted me to do?" asked Derek, incredulously.

Max gave his brother a quick, cynical glance and began to walk up and down the room, hands in his pockets, his face puckered.

"Curiously enough, it *is*."

"You would like to have seen me *marry* Lucinda, no matter what she was?"

"What she *was* is not necessarily what she *is*, today."

"Okay—that's why I told her I'd forget it. *I* didn't break the engagement, remember. *She* did."

Again Max eyed his half-brother.

"You told her you'd *forgive* her."

"Yes, and Mrs. Brill-Burrie said she thought I'd been very generous. But I must say since I have spoken to Vivian I'm not as upset about losing Lucinda as I was when she first broke it off. I feel I've been spared something."

In that split second after his brother had spoken, it struck Max Chalmerson that whatever he, Max, had done to help bring about this situation, he would regret it all his life. And even more would he regret the way Derek had accepted Vivian's word against Lucinda's.

He suddenly turned on the boy:

"You self-righteous little fool!"

Derek stood stock-still, his fair face crimsoning, his mouth gaping open.

"I . . . you . . . *well*, of all the . . ." he stammered and stopped.

Max went on:

"Yes, that's what I said, *self-righteous fool!* I would have thought more of you if you'd stood by the girl no matter what *I* felt—or said about her. No matter even if I had begged you on my bended knees to give her up. I'd have been prouder of you if you'd stuck by her."

Derek gasped. He had just been given two strong gins by Vivian Brill-Burrie and he was still under her influence. She cast a definite spell—that sweet, sad, smooth personality that she could produce at will, and which had misled quite a number of men—until they saw through her. All his life, Derek had revered and looked up to his half-brother. But he was not going to be called a self-righteous fool, even by Max. He snapped:

"Mrs. Brill-Burrie said that Lucinda could always charm the hind legs off a donkey. I've been the donkey for a long time. Now maybe you're one. Obviously Lucinda has got at *you*."

Max opened his mouth as though to make a furious retort, then closed it again. He picked up the hat and gloves which he had just thrown on the bed.

"I don't think we'd better carry this much further, Derek. It's gone far enough. I did what I thought was right when I asked Lucinda to tell you about her past. Now it's just a question of whether you're well-rid of her, or she is well-rid of *you*."

"Look here——" began Derek.

"I'm through," Max interrupted.

"Well, this is a nice thing," stammered Derek, "to l-let Lucinda come between us like this."

"I accept a certain amount of blame," said Max, "although you'd have heard about it all from Vivian, anyhow. But I reckon you'd have shown up as a better man if you'd been more generous to Lucinda."

"I tell you it was *she* who broke with *me*," said Derek, hotly.

Max shook his head.

"It struck me when I talked to Lucinda that she had some pride. I'm convinced now that she has plenty of it—and guts as well. Also I certainly can't now accuse her of husband-hunting, otherwise she would have humbly accepted the forgiveness you offered."

Derek, who had never been a very stable character, felt Vivian's influence weakening and Max's gaining strength. He said, feebly:

"Oh, God, what do you think I ought to do now, Max? I don't want to do the wrong thing."

"I reckon we've both of us done that already," said Max.

"Shall I try and see her?"

"I don't suppose she'd see you. But I have every intention of trying to see her, myself. Will you kindly give me her address?"

Derek stared, open-mouthed.

"What can *you* possibly have to say to Lucinda under the circumstances?"

Max repeated:

"Her address, please, Derek."

Derek wrote it down and handed the slip of paper to his brother.

"What are you going to say?" he repeated, doubtfully.

"Make my apologies to her first of all," said Max, "then what you two choose to do afterwards is your affair."

He left Derek gasping.

But a further shock awaited Max. When Mr. Mace opened the front door of the house in Putney to the tall, handsome young man from Kenya and recognised him, his face froze.

"Why have you come here, Mr. Chalmerson?" he asked.

"To see Lucinda, if I may," said Max.

"I'm sorry," said Lucinda's father. "She isn't here."

"Do you expect her——?" began Max. Mr. Mace interrupted.

"You and your brother, between you, have ruined my girl's life, Mr. Chalmerson. I wonder you have the nerve to come to this house."

2

Do not affix postage stamps if posted in Gt. Britain, Channel Islands or Northern Ireland

BUSINESS REPLY SERVICE
LICENCE NO. KE 2450

CORONET ROMANCE CLUB

St. Paul's House

Warwick Lane

LONDON

EC4B 4HB

Max stared, feeling hot and embarrassed. Mr. Mace eyed him with bitterness.

"We were all so happy last night till you came back from abroad with that abominable story—raking up old scandals and lies—allowing that fiendish woman to come between Cindy and Derek. Well, I hope you're satisfied. Cindy arrived home about an hour ago, in a *terrible* state, packed a case and went off. Neither her mother nor I could stop her."

Max felt more than embarrassed now. His pulses jerked in a most unpleasant fashion.

"But where has she gone, Mr. Mace?"

"*You* tell *me*," said Mr. Mace in the same bitter voice. "We don't know. Her mother is almost demented. Cindy just said she wouldn't stay in Putney one hour longer and that she had finished with love and marriage and everything else. She gave us no address—no clue as to where she might be going. She just went. And we hold YOU to blame."

9

THERE had been several occasions in Max Chalmerson's life
when he had faced danger—particularly during that last trip
up country in Kenya across parched land devastated by
drought—when he was trying to deal with animals maddened
by their intolerable thirst.

He could remember one particular occasion when he and
two of the native boys had come suddenly upon a lion. So
suddenly that Max had not had time to move the safety catch
on his rifle and pull the trigger. The lion crouched for the
leap. Max had to act in a split second; found himself scaling a
tree, scrambling for dear life up to safety with his two boys
jittering at him from opposite branches. Max had felt sick.
His hands had shaken. He had known that he was scared.
A man might well be scared, with a rifle that had jammed and
a hungry lion within fifty yards of him.

This morning in Putney, facing an irate father, Max felt a
different sort of sickness and a different kind of fear. Not for
himself but for a girl; the young lovely girl who might have
been his sister-in-law. And he was afraid because she had
disappeared; and of what she might do. Afraid, too, because
he had woken up to the full belief that she was innocent.

It would have been better, he knew, if in the first place he
had used what influence he had to shut Vivian Brill-Burrie's
mouth and left the two youngsters alone. Oh, God! he was
sorry. He could kick himself. Mentally he did so and without
mercy. He spoke in a low voice to Lucinda's father—the
tired-looking business-man whose own face was so anxious.
They were *all* afraid for Lucinda. And they none of them
dared put a name to that fear.

Then Mr. Mace spoke:

"I'll say goodbye——"

"Wait a minute," said Max, quickly.

"I see no useful purpose in our prolonging the conversation," said the older man, stiffly.

"Look—I know it seems as though I'm primarily to blame but this would have happened whatever I did. Mrs. Brill-Burrie herself was determined to spill that story."

"Oh, yes, we had enough of her two years ago," said Arthur Mace. "She tried to ruin Cindy then. She's got a perverted mind, that woman. She's eaten up by vanity and jealousy. It was her jealousy of our young pretty Cindy that made her start the whole show. Her own husband came here and cleared Cindy's name. We believed him. I think you've behaved atrociously, Mr. Chalmerson, and your brother worse. No doubt you acted from a mistaken sense of loyalty to Derek. But he showed none toward my poor little girl."

"I'm damned sorry, Mr. Mace. Believe it or not—I wish Derek had behaved otherwise. I've just told him so."

"Well, it's too late."

"But what are you going to do about Lucinda? Where do you think she's gone?"

Mr. Mace passed a hand wearily across his forehead.

"We had hoped that she had gone to her godmother but Lady Hordham has neither seen nor heard from her. She is just as upset and indignant as we are. Cindy merely told us she wanted to get right away from everybody she knew. She asked her mother to phone the place where she works to say she is ill. This thing has hit her really hard, you know."

"Oh, God," muttered Max.

When Arthur Mace had first opened the door to Derek's half-brother he had felt hostile and unwilling to speak to him. Now, feeling less antagonistic, he saw for himself that the elder Chalmerson brother was honestly sorry for what had happened. Cindy was, after all, nothing to do with him. It was quite decent of him to have come round. Gruffly, Mr. Mace said:

"You seem to be doing Derek's job. Why hasn't *he* come to see me?"

Max agreed.

"It's a bit awkward for the boy, I suppose. I'm not really defending him but his mind was poisoned by that woman. *And* Lucinda broke the engagement. Derek is completely *bouleversé*. But I'm quite sure that if we can find Lucinda, we can put this thing right for the pair of them."

"You can take it from me that my daughter will never have anything more to do with Derek," Mr. Mace said coldly.

"Well, I intend to find her," said Max, "if I spend the rest of my leave in England doing so."

Now Arthur Mace stared.

"But why——?"

"I have my reasons," cut in Max.

"Then you don't believe she was guilty?"

A moment's hesitation, then Max said slowly:

"*No, I don't. And I'm damned sorry I ever did.*"

Mr. Mace sighed.

"Well, I don't know how we're going to find the poor girl. It's most worrying. We've tried everything. Her friend Iris Turnbull—anybody we imagine might have a line on where she's gone. No one has seen or heard from her."

"Did she give *you*, her parents, no hint at all as to where she was going?"

Mr. Mace shook his head. Then:

"Look, you'd better come in, Chalmerson, and talk to my wife. It's no good standing out there on the doorstep."

"Thanks," said Max gratefully. "I'd like that very much."

It was two o'clock before he returned to his hotel. Derek was still there up in Max's room—half sitting, half lying on the bed, smoking. He looked pallid and miserable but Max felt no sympathy. He said:

"Had any lunch?"

"No."

"Neither have I. I've been walking for the last hour or two. We'd better go downstairs and order tea."

Derek got off the bed and looked gloomily at his half-brother.

"Did you see Lucinda?"

"No, she's cleared off. Nobody knows where she is."

"Oh, lord!" muttered Derek. He moistened his lips with the tip of his tongue. He had had a bad session here alone with his thoughts of Lucinda. One half of him felt desperately ashamed of the way he had treated her. The other half, bolstered up by Vivian Brill-Burrie, continued to argue that he had acted very fairly and generously. After all, it was a 'bit much' that he should have been expected to believe every word she said. It should have been enough for her to accept his forgiveness and carry on with the engagement. But of course she had been right when she had said that he might always wonder what *had* happened between her and Brill-Burrie . . .

But now he felt worried.

"You don't think—her people don't think she will do anything foolish? That would be ghastly."

"Yes, it would be ghastly," said Max.

During tea he told Derek about his interview with the Maces. Derek listened miserably. He couldn't really see why Max should make him feel that he, Derek, was to blame for everything. *His* conscience was clear. After all, it was damned bad luck on *him* that Lucinda should have earned herself such a reputation (whether she fully deserved it or not). But when he began to argue this way, Max shut him up.

"We look at these things from different viewpoints," he said. "Once and for all, let me explain my attitude, Derry. The last thing I wished was for you to marry the wrong sort of girl and I admit I was anxious that you should tell Lucinda what you'd heard, then hear what she had to say. But it was never at any time a foregone conclusion in my mind that you would throw her over. I only wanted you to start even. But that's over. Let's get down to the present. *I* believe in Lucinda. *You* don't."

"Well you can't altogether blame me——" Derek began to mumble.

"Oh, shut up, Derry, you make me sick."

"You've changed very suddenly—you seem to be entirely on Lucinda's side."

"One is entitled to change one's opinions."

"What do you want me to do then? Help find Lucinda and beg her on my bended knees to forgive *me* for offering to forgive *her*?"

Max shook his head, looking at Derek through half-shut eyes, much as he would have looked at a new animal that he had just discovered. He really hadn't known Derek very well until now—he realised that. What a fantastically stubborn, even *stupid* streak there was in the boy. How little he understood human beings.

"For the love of mike, Derry, drop this 'holier-than-thou' attitude," he snapped.

Derek lowered his gaze.

"Oh, very well, what do you want me to do?"

"Look," said Max. "The Maces are naturally very bitter about you and they don't very much like the part I've played in this show. But I think they do believe that I sincerely regret it and that I want to help."

"How can you?"

"Well, the first thing is to find Lucinda. She can't be allowed to roam round on her own, feeling that her future husband has walked out on her and that life's finished for her, and all that. Her own mother says she's very sensitive and easily hurt."

"It's just a question of one woman's word against another's, isn't it?" muttered Derek, filling his pipe. "I mean Vivian Brill-Burrie against Lucinda."

"I've already decided which woman I believe."

Derek raised his head and looked at his brother with astonishment.

"I thought you were *keen* on Vivian. She seems to think——"

"Then she thinks wrong," cut in Max. "I was sorry for

her out in Nairobi but I'm not any more. I don't like spiteful females."

"Then why didn't you scotch her story in the first place?" exclaimed Derek.

"*Touché*," said Max. "I couldn't agree with you more. That's what I should have done. I made too much of feeling I ought to look after my little brother. Now I see he can take care of himself."

"I don't know what you're inferring and I don't see why we must quarrel over Lucinda."

"Then we won't," said Max. "We'll just go our own ways. Mine lies in the direction of Lucinda. I'm frightened for that girl. I've got to find her."

"Then I suppose I ought to try and find her, too."

"No," said Max, and signalled to a passing waiter for his bill. "I reckon it might be better if you kept out of it."

"Look here, Max, this is all getting a bit beyond me."

"I'm quite sure it is," said Max with a not very pleasant smile. "That's why I am going to do the job for you."

"I don't understand you."

"And you don't understand what you've done to that girl, either. She expected you to stand by her."

"Oh, I do think she was genuinely fond of me," said Derek pompously.

Now Max snarled at him:

"And how fond were *you* of *her*? God! You really do make me sick."

He got up and walked out of the lounge. Derek followed.

"Where are you going, Max?"

"To see Iris Turnbull. I've already tried once but she was out. Her boy friend has taken her out to lunch. Mrs. Turnbull said they'd be in by six. Girls who are close friends tell each other things they don't always tell their parents. I think with a little cross-examination I might be able to get Iris to give me a clue as to where Lucinda is hiding."

"Do you want me to drive you there?" asked Derek.

"No, thanks. You'd better keep out of this for the moment. I began this unfortunate affair and if I can put it right it's up to me to do so."

"But I'm sorry you think so badly of me, Max!"

"If it's any consolation to you, my dear Derek, I feel just as badly about myself. I'll let you know what goes on. By the way, you might do me a service. Ring Mrs. Brill-Burrie and tell her I'm extremely sorry I must cancel my dinner with her tonight. Say I've been called out of town on business. Anything you like."

Derek watched his brother go up in the lift to his bedroom. Then he left the hotel. He had parked *Mr. Moses* in a side street. Even the sight of his veteran car could not cheer Derek up. And the ring—the little engagement ring Cindy had thrown at him—seemed to burn a hole in his pocket.

Suddenly he felt extremely lonely. It hit him with a bang that he was no longer engaged to the most beautiful girl in the world, and that his marriage would not now take place. Also that he would never have this home he and Cindy had planned. That was—not unless Max found her and brought her back and everything came right again.

As he drove away from Sloane Square, Derek kept arguing with himself in an obstinate way.

'*I offered to forgive her, didn't I? A lot of men in my place might have been suspicious. It's all rot this business of Max saying I would have believed in her if I'd really loved her. He's never been in love. How should he know? I think he's behaving rottenly to me.*'

Derek tried to console himself with the thought that Max was behaving rottenly. Also that he, Derek, had been misjudged; badly treated by both Lucinda *and* Max.

Then Derek remembered one place where he would be welcome and made to feel that his actions were justified. He wouldn't telephone Vivian Brill-Burrie on his brother's behalf. He'd go and see her, personally.

10

THE lighthouse fascinated Lucinda.

Every morning she would stand at the window of the cottage on the edge of the cliff and look down at the splendid structure, five hundred feet below. The seemingly immovable lighthouse that had been built on solid rock around which the waves moved perpetually and the seagulls screamed and wheeled, their wings flashing in the sunlight as they encircled the intricate tower.

Every night she watched the revolving light break the darkness of the water and shed fantastically powerful beams beyond the reefs, warning the ships of danger. At first she found good weather down here. But during the last twenty-four hours there had been a change. It was grey and cloudy today.

Lucinda had been here for nearly three weeks, living in the whitewashed coastguard's cottage. Summer was ending. The skies were stormy. The blue-green Atlantic had darkened to a metallic grey, flecked by white-horses and the snow of the foam that sprayed into the air as the waves dashed and hissed around the base of the lighthouse.

The old coastguard had warned Lucinda this morning.

"'Tis blowing up for a gale. 'Ee mustn't go too near cliff-edge, Missie."

But Lucinda didn't mind going near the edge of the cliff. She had a head for heights. There was something about this place that held her in a kind of thrall. The tremendous expanse of sea and sky and the loneliness appealed to her greatly in the present circumstances.

This morning, wearing slacks, jersey and a short duffle coat, for it was several degrees cooler and the wind had an edge to it, she walked over the green springy turf in the direction of the village. She had a letter to post. A letter to her mother. The only person in the world to whom she had written since she had run away from home.

'Run-away' was the word, she thought somewhat ironically. She even felt that she had been a coward to come so far, and stay away so long. But something kept her down here; something stronger than herself. Maybe it was the very potency and ruthlessness of the Cornish coast that appealed to her. So here she still was, in mid-September, a few miles from Penzance in this tiny village of St. Ruthen, living with the old retired coastguard and his wife.

She had a tiny bedroom—a mere attic under the eaves with a casement window from which she could look down on the wonderful sea. It was a revelation to her; like the rest of this Cornish territory. Far removed from the crowded cities and the better-known villages, St. Ruthen was one of the few remaining 'hide-outs'; possibly unpopular because the beach was inaccessible; there were no sands for children, and bathing was impossible. There was no shelter from the wind—the perpetual wind that seemed to blow, whether lightly and warmly in the summer months, or with devastating fury in the winter. The wind which depressed her in London exhilarated her down here.

She posted her letter and bought some cigarettes in the tiny shop that was both post-office and grocer. Ever since she had left home she had written in much the same vein to her parents. She was very well; absolutely content so long as they left her alone and nobody tried to follow her.

As she retraced her footsteps, Lucinda considered how completely her life had changed since she and Derek parted.

When she had first rushed away from him it had been with the intention of spending only one week alone. She had come straight to Penzance where lived an old servant who had been with her parents in their 'palmy days'; and who had always been devoted to 'Little Cindy'. Old Jess, now eighty and partially blind, had a tiny flat in Penzance but the town

was crowded even at this time of the year. So Lucinda only
spent one night with Jess. Some friends of hers—Alice and
Tom Trevanna at St. Ruthen—had offered Lucinda asylum.
When she first saw their isolated, white-washed cottage, she
fell in love with it. It was just what she needed. A retreat
from the world, where she could reorientate herself. The wind
and the sea would heal her. She felt in fact like a bird whose
wings were bruised and who could no longer fly without pain.
She had experienced such pain as she could hardly bear. She
had felt revolted by the very idea of love and loving when she
first got down here. But after a week with the Trevannas she
felt so much better, she wanted to stay on.

   She put a call through to Monsieur Ruchelle of Knightsbridge and explained the situation. His first thought was to
get her back at once, but the mere idea of returning to the
show-rooms to model dresses or try to please difficult customers made Lucinda wish to run a mile. She reminded
Monsieur that she was due for a fortnight's holiday and had
been going on her honeymoon. It had been suggested that she
continued to do a half-day's work with Ruchelle once she was
married to Derek. (He had been willing for her to do so for a
time, anyhow. They were a modern couple, and neither of
them averse to a working partnership.) But now she told
Monsieur that if he wanted her back at all, he must extend her
leave. He—out of honest admiration for her, backed up by
Madame who was very attached to Lucinda—generously gave
her the extra holiday. On full pay, too—so Lucinda had no
qualms about staying away and having to ask her parents for
financial help. But she would not give them an address.
She made it clear that if they looked at the postmark and came
in search of her, it would be a wasted journey. She would
refuse to go home—until she was ready.

   In all her life, Lucinda had never felt a greater need for
being alone. Only immediately after that unpleasant episode
with Dr. Brill-Burrie had she felt so beaten. But even then,
she had wanted to hold her head high and fight on. But

Derek's lack of faith in her had been such a heavy blow that it had taken from her even her wish to fight. It was that sense of defeat, as much as her genuine grief at losing Derek, that had brought her so low. She felt raw with the humiliation and bitterness.

Her parents had so far respected her wish to be left in peace and she knew that as long as they could be certain she was in no danger, they would go on respecting it. As for Derek—she was quite sure *he* would not come in search of her, because she had told her mother to let him know that she would never, never have anything more to do with him.

The thought of brother Max did not bother her at all, even though she believed that all the trouble had started through him. She remembered Max only with resentment and she took it for granted that *he* would not mind that she had disappeared. He would soon be returning to Kenya. She would not see him again.

The longer she lived in St. Ruthen, however, sequestered from the world, speaking only to the old Cornish couple who had given her a room, the more she felt her former joy of living renewed within her. The sap began to rise again—the sap of new courage, of steadfast belief in God—of acute dislike of all the petty tyrannies and restrictions of ordinary, everyday social life. Down here in Cornwall she could no longer even feel troubled by the malice and spite of such a woman as Vivian Brill-Burrie. She no longer loved Derek. But it was the loss of her love and faith that had brought her so low. This stage had now passed. She had begun to feel a sense of responsibility for her misfortunes. It was her own behaviour that had brought this cataclysm about her ears. How could she ever have been such a pleasure-loving, stupid little idiot, she asked herself, dismayed.

Each day she went for long, lonely walks along the cliffs or spent hours watching the sea-birds, the ever-changing marvels of the Atlantic ocean swirling around the base of the lighthouse. It fascinated her. She began to feel that if there were such splendours, such nobility in nature, there must also exist these exalted qualities in the soul of man. There should be no room for *littleness*. Life should be led with great purpose toward an ideal. She even asked herself how she was ever going to exchange this new existence, with its extraordinary mental illumination and peace, for the trivial life she had led in the past. But she realised that she could not remain on such a high plane. The air was too rarefied for a warm-hearted, impulsive girl like Lucinda.

Then she met Barry. The tall, fair-haired, blue-eyed young lighthouse-keeper who was in charge of the great lantern-gallery; the lights and the reflectors. He was a nephew of Tom Trevanna. He did so many hours on duty for so many days and weeks, then came ashore. Whilst ashore this time he met and talked with the girl whom his uncle called 'our young lady from Lunnon'.

Lucinda was in no mood to encourage the attention of any man in the ordinary sense. But Barry was a person whom she soon found she *could* admit into her daily life and whose company she rapidly grew to appreciate. It was, in fact, young Barry who drew her away from the over-spiritualised border-line—this state of sublimation which she had been trying to acquire. He brought her back to complete normality again. He was such a down-to-earth, practical, delightful fellow—full of good humour. Twenty-three, unmarried, unattached, he had given his life so far to this work for which he had been trained.

He told Lucinda when he first met her how the lighthouse had become the breath of life to him. She felt that she understood. It was a worthwhile job. But Barry was no fanatic. He was a handsome, flesh-and-blood young Cornishman. Usually slow to make friends, he seemed to thaw quickly in Lucinda's company. He found he could pour out his heart to her. She learned how he had been orphaned as a small boy; how he had had one girl friend from Penzance but she preferred the gay lights and the dance-halls and married a publican. But Barry openly declared that he fully intended to find another love one day, get married and have children. That, he said, was man's destiny on earth. To have the right woman at his side and 'a pack of kids'. The lighthouse was his only love now, yes, he said, and a man's job must come first but only *until* he married. Then he must give most of himself to his wife and his family.

Lucinda had listened to this philosophy, entranced. When she congratulated him on his outlook, and maintained that some girl was going to be lucky, Barry gave her his bright boyish smile and winked in the friendly way which she could not possibly find offensive.

"Reckon that's so, and once I find her I'll bring her to *you* for inspection. I reckon you know a lot about girls and the world. And I reckon I know nothing—after my let-down, Miss Lucinda."

"Well, I don't know much more," was her answer, and the sadness in her eyes had its source in her heart. He little knew how she had failed in *her* love-life. She sighed. There was something about this fair, blue-eyed young man that reminded her of Derek—and their happier moments together. Oh, how she wished Derek hadn't behaved so badly. But he was weak— she knew that now. Barry had strength. And the strong, thoroughly masculine side of him reminded her not of Derek *but of Max*; the half-brother, who had such a much more powerful personality.

She felt uneasy suddenly, and said goodbye to Barry. But she continued to meet and talk to him. Without in the least wanting it to happen, she gradually saw how things between them were shaping. It was Alice Trevanna who sounded the warning bell.

"You'm a proper fascination to our young Barry. Him can't keep away from you, Miss," she teased the young London lady.

Lucinda coloured and answered with a laugh:

"Oh, surely not. It's the lighthouse that your nephew is so keen on. That's why he comes here so often."

But the new light in Barry's blue eyes distressed more than flattered Lucinda when he came to the cottage again. She could swear that she saw his hand shake as he lighted her cigarette for her. She didn't want this to happen. It was too soon, following her unhappy engagement. Besides, although she admired and liked this boy, she could never fall in love with him. He wasn't her kind. He was too 'raw'. Not at all her type.

This was the day before Barry's leave ashore came to an end.

"Reckon I'll be thinking a lot upon you, Miss Lucinda," he said, sadly.

"Oh, it's been a wonderful fortnight for me, and thanks for everything, Barry," she said lightly.

"You're not happy, though, are you, Miss Lucinda?" he went on, and added abruptly: "Reckon I'd like to try to do something for you if you'd let me."

He was so humble and charming, and seemed so very much younger rather than older than herself that she felt toward him almost like an elder sister. If he was really in love with her she was sure he would never say so. He would consider it 'cheeky' because he was only a lad of the village. Having suffered in love herself she felt sorry for him—unwilling that he should suffer through her. She said:

"No, there isn't anything you can do for me, Barry."

"I haven't offended you, have I?" he asked, anxiously.

"No, of course not."

He looked at her. She was so far above him he felt that she was like an inaccessible star which he wanted to worship. He knew nothing of her own story although she had once hinted that she had been engaged, then broken it off. Any man that had had a chance to marry Miss Lucinda and then lost it must be a fool in Barry's estimation. He said nervously:

"It's my last day ashore, Miss Lucinda. Won't you come out with me this afternoon?"

Then as she hesitated, he implored:

"Please can't I take you out to tea somewhere?"

Now she broke into the frank, fresh laughter which had been silent for so long. She answered:

"To have a Cornish tea—splits and cream and jam? Oh, dear me, no. I'll put on too much weight. But I'll tell you something I *would* like to do, Barry. I'd adore to go out on the sea with you. I've become so mad about this sea of yours and I know I'm a good sailor. When I was a little girl my father had a boat and everybody used to be seasick except me."

"I could get the use of a little motor-boat owned by a friend of mine but I reckon the swell might upset you, Miss."

"Couldn't we just go round the point—Mussel Rock—isn't that what it's called, over there?"

She pointed to a small, sharp promontory of wet black rocks. It had a bluish tinge from the mussels thickly encrusted upon it. The water creamed and lapped around it throwing jets of crystalline spray up into the air.

"I've always been fascinated to know what lies around the corner," she said.

"Just a bit of beach, Miss Lucinda, which can never be reached except at the spring tides. Then folks can climb over the rocks when the tide's out but mainly it's visitors who go there taking no notice of the sign that bathing is dangerous."

"Let us go round by sea and see it. We could also go as far as you think safe, out toward the lighthouse—my beloved, fascinating lighthouse."

"I believe you really love it, Miss Lucinda."

"I do," she said. "I *do*!"

And the thought suddenly struck her that a man's love should be like that lighthouse—built on solid rock, immovable, powerful, secure, making a woman feel the light and warmth of such safety.

She thought, inexplicably, in the same second, of Max Chalmerson, but tossed the thought aside in sudden bitterness. She had left London hating him. She would always hate him.

Suddenly she flung her arms above her head. The wind blew her hair about cheeks that had grown deliciously brown from the sun and the strong air, and were free from all make-up. She looked glorious in the eyes of the simple, Cornish boy; lissom, tall, infinitely graceful. She touched her lips with her tongue and savoured the salt of the blowing spume. She had never felt so well or so buoyant in all her life; that life which had taken on an entirely new meaning. Yet something was still missing. She did not know what, but she did know that she wanted to *live*. She had been spiritually restored by her sojourn here and somehow Barry, the young lighthouse-keeper, had made her feel that one's work and one's personal emotional life should count after all. One must not for ever shut oneself away, as nuns in a convent, from the tribulations and difficulties of the outside world.

Tomorrow she would go back to London, perhaps. She was finished with Derek, with Max and with the past. She would never allow Vivian—or anyone—to hurt her again.

She was seized suddenly with some of the devil-may-care and bravado of the younger Cindy—the mischief-loving, reckless, importunate Cindy. Breathlessly she said:

"Come on, Barry—let's do something quite mad, like taking the boat out slap through a mountainous wave, even if we have to swim for shore!"

Barry laughed. His eyes were bright with admiration. The strong character, the vivid personality of this young lady from London was unique, and irresistible to him. So far was he fascinated that he did indeed take her out later on in a small strong boat which had an outboard motor. The sea was growing rougher now, whipped by the rising wind. He felt quite capable of handling the boat and meant to keep near the shore, but he wouldn't have taken out any other girl but Miss Lucinda.

She sat facing him with a yellow rubber fisherman's coat over her, and a sou'wester on her head. She was very happy. She felt this to be an adventure. She felt insignificant, too, and even a little over-awed on such a tremendous sea, under the tremendous expanse of sky whilst the grey gulls wheeled and screeched overhead. She found it difficult to turn her gaze away from the lighthouse. Oh, how strong and beautiful it was! She envied the young keeper who would be going out there tomorrow to his lonely job in the company of two other men who, like himself, were dedicated to the service.

"The tide's turning. Better get back, Miss Lucinda," said Barry.

"Oh, not yet," she pleaded. "Let's tie up on that little beach under Mussel Rock—just for a moment. It looks so lonely—heavenly!"

She had forgotten how this boy felt about her. She was blind to the adoration in his eyes. The old reckless spirit was still upon her. If she was to return to London tomorrow and go home to start the old sedate life again, she felt she must cram every possible glorious experience into this day—before it all ended.

The rain had started to spatter from a darkening sky. Barry frowned up at it.

"Sou'wester's freshening, Miss Lucinda."

"Are we in danger?" she laughed.

"N-no," he said, doubtfully, "but reckon I ought to take you back."

"The beach—just for a moment. I want to climb up Mussel Rock and feel I've stood there. It's been my ambition. Please, Barry."

He could not resist her. He steered the boat into the small sheltered bay where for a moment they could be secure from the swell of the waves and the whine of the wind. She sprang out—she had put on waders to please Barry—and dragged her legs through the creaming waves on to the wet rocks. A flock of gulls rose into the air and broke the silence with their wild screaming. Lucinda experienced a strange ecstasy as she climbed on to the top of the rocks and stood there as she had long wanted to do, the rain drenching her face, her gaze fixed on the lighthouse. Tonight she would watch those revolving rays for the last time. For the last time they would flash into her little attic bedroom, then sweep away, leaving her in darkness. What had led her down here? she wondered. Not only the wish to get away and seek shelter with old Jess. Some more powerful whim of Fate had brought her to St. Ruthen. Into what shape was her life being moulded now? She wished she knew the answer. But none came and suddenly her crazy elation vanished. She felt lost, even scared by the thought of the future. It was with deep depression that she remembered the mistakes she had made when she was a 'teenager' and all the disastrous consequences of such follies. By now she should have been married to Derek. Once he had seemed so dear to her—so very necessary. She felt utterly lost and alone here on this rock, with the waves thundering below her. Every human being was alone, she thought, and must map out his own destiny. For most women, the greatest need was to be loved. She, Lucinda, needed love, too. She had lost it all when she lost Derek. Would it ever be possible to find it again? Supposing when she got back to London, he came in search of her and begged her to give him another chance, *would she give it to him? Did she want him back?* But like a flash there came into her mind the remembrance of Max's face—the handsome, ironical eyes of Max who had come between her and her dream of love.

What was it *he* had said to her at their last meeting? She had said to him: '*Most women need security*' and he had answered:

'*And you especially. It's something you've always lacked, isn't it?*'

That ice-cold truth had hit her hard at the time. The thought of it shook her again in this psychic moment of re-discovering, re-shaping her shattered emotions. She clenched her hands. Why couldn't she forget Max? Why must it always be *Max* rather than Derek, who flayed her memories?

Then she heard Barry's voice calling to her:

"Miss Lucinda!"

She looked down at him and waved. But he did not wave back. He was standing by the boat, his hands on the tiller.

"What is it?" she shouted.

"Come down, please, Miss Lucinda. We've run into trouble."

"What sort of trouble?"

"Bad, Miss Lucinda. Engine's petered out and I can't get her to start . . ."

It was at this precise moment that Max Chalmerson, driving a small sports-car from London, reached Penzance after a run which he had started soon after midnight. He had pulled up at a pub for a meal. He was sick of the long trek to the West Country. The traffic was still heavy, despite the fact that the summer season had ended. No use having a fast car like the one he had hired, he reflected crossly. One just couldn't get on.

He had thought it was going to be fine but clouds were rolling up and the wind was rising. He didn't really like the look of the weather. However, he was not far from St. Ruthen now. The A.A. had told him how to reach this out-of-the-way spot. And while he snatched his meal, Max's mind reverted to a telephone conversation which he had had with Iris Turnbull last night.

"When you first came to see me," she said, "I didn't feel at all inclined to help you find Cindy. I thought you, as well as Derek, had treated her badly. But you have convinced me that all you want to do is to establish her good reputation and try to put things right for her. How you're going to do it, I don't know. But I *can*, I think, tell you now where to find her."

For the last two and a half weeks, Max had been hanging around London in a state of restrained irritation and considerable anxiety. All his efforts, and the few feeble ones made by Derek, to discover Lucinda's whereabouts, had failed.

The wish to see her again was fast becoming an obsession with Max. If he had really helped to hurt her he must undo that hurt if he was to live with his own conscience peaceably in the future.

He had rung her parents once or twice only to draw a blank. But Lucinda's friend, Iris, seemed to be on his side. *She* was so troubled about Lucinda that she was only too willing to help him trace her.

"I went to see Aunt Angela—Mrs. Mace—this afternoon," Iris had told him. "Before she came into the room, I just happened to see a letter in Lucinda's handwriting lying on the desk. I'm sure I wasn't meant to see it but curiosity made me pick it up and look at the postmark. It was 'St. Ruthen'."

"Where's that?" demanded Max, eagerly.

"Not many miles out of Penzance. Christopher looked it all up for me."

"I'm deeply grateful," said Max. "I can soon find out where she is staying."

"Don't give me away," Iris begged. "I saw Aunt Angela snatch the letter and hide it as soon as she came into the room. I know she'd be upset if she thought I'd read it. But I just can't understand why she hasn't told *me* that she knows where poor darling Cindy is, or what she's doing. I suppose Cindy told her not to. But I think she's been away too long alone. I'm worried. I wonder Derek isn't crazy with remorse. I don't understand him."

"I'm only just beginning to understand the boy," said Max a trifle grimly, "but he's out of this. It is between you and myself, Iris. I shall hire a car at once and go straight down to St. Ruthen."

II

It was a bad squall—the worst they had had on the Cornish coast for years. It seemed that there was only a short interval between light-grey skies and moderate winds, then a great scurrying mass of black storm clouds and a howling gale.

By four o'clock—long after Lucinda and the young light-house-keeper should have been back at the cottage for tea—Barry's shouting had drawn the attention of a passing villager who heard the cries and gathered that young Barry and Mrs. Trevanna's London lodger were in difficulties down by Mussel Rock. A short while afterward the coastguards arrived with their life-saving apparatus. And by that time, too, half the village of St. Ruthen had gathered—men in oilskins and sou'westers—women in macintoshes with waterproof hoods, all peering anxiously over the cliff whilst rumours spread fast from one to another.

"'Tis Barry and that young girl, who looks like a model . . ."

"'Tis said that young Barry's keen on she . . ."

"They say boat won't start and tide caught 'em so they can't get round Point . . ."

Then it was that a tall stranger whom St. Ruthen had never seen down here before arrived—pushed his way through the crowd and leaned more anxiously than the others over the cliff. He wore a short macintosh. The heavy rain had plastered his thick dark hair against his bare head. His hand-some face was grim.

Max Chalmerson had already discovered where Lucinda was staying. At the same time he found out that she had just been caught by the tide and was down there in that dangerous little cove with a young lighthouse-keeper named Barry.

How typical, Max had thought a trifle ironically, that he should discover Cindy not only in the teeth of a storm but as the centre of publicity. She seemed fated to get herself talked about.

The coastguards, busy with their ropes, ordered Max to go back.

"It is unsafe to get too close to edge in this wind, zurr."

"Are they all right?" he shouted.

"Barry is, but t'young lady's been hurt."

Max felt his pulses jerk with dismay.

"Hurt? How? Do you mean badly?"

Nobody could tell him much but the coastguard thought that one of the mountainous waves must have knocked Lucinda against a rock and stunned her. It was not long before the young couple were up on the cliff safe and sound; Barry none the worse but looking extremely sheepish, and refusing to explain away his foolhardiness in having taken the boat out to Mussel Rock in this weather. Mr. and Mrs. Trevanna arrived. The woman was shocked and distressed as she saw the unconscious Miss Lucinda being laid on a rug upon the grass, and hastened home to build up the fire and get hot-water bottles. There was some talk of sending for an ambulance to take Lucinda to hospital.

Max knelt beside the unconscious girl and lifted one of her cold wet hands. This was a Lucinda he had never expected to see—a half-drowned nymph, drenched in salt-water, her lovely hair sodden, her face colourless, her eyes shut. Blood oozed from a cut on her right temple where there showed already the swell of a bruise.

Barry was agonised. He felt that the whole thing was his fault and tried to mutter an apology to Max whom he presumed was a relative of Lucinda's.

"Reckon I'm nothing but a fool," he said. "But I didn't expect motor-boat to go wrong. I tried everything to get the engine going, then t'storm broke. It was more than unfortunate."

"It was," said Max curtly, and chafed Lucinda's hands between his strong fingers. Then, looking up at the circle of inquisitive faces, he added: "I think I'll carry her straight home. She's no weight for me."

The crowd separated and made room for the big tall man. The girls admired his magnificent figure as he lifted Lucinda up in his arms as though she were a child.

At that moment Lucinda's lashes lifted. To Max's relief she regained consciousness if only for a second. Her eyes, dazed at first, then startled, gave him a long unbelieving look. The colour swept back into her cheeks.

"*Max!*" she whispered, incredulously.

"Yes. You're all right now, my dear. Don't worry," he said. She made a feeble effort to struggle on to her feet.

"Let me go at once——" she began, but before she could say any more she had drifted back into insensibility.

When she fully recovered a few hours later she found herself in her little attic bedroom, hot-water bottles at her feet and back and the local doctor who visited St. Ruthen twice a week, sitting beside her. For the second time she also became aware of Max. He was standing at the foot of her bed.

Once more she felt angry and yet . . . unwilling though she was to admit it . . . she found the sight of him exciting. She seemed to have been so long alone amongst strangers. Max came direct from home. She felt that she knew him even better than she actually did, but what he was doing here she could not imagine. She turned to Dr. Polmerrow. He was a youngish man with glasses and a receding chin and no great air of brilliance but he was able to reassure Lucinda—and those who were worried about her—that there was no cause for anxiety. She had only been slightly concussed. He had dressed her forehead but he wanted her to stay in bed a couple of days. She was naturally 'shocked'. He prescribed some tranquillising tablets and a sleeping pill for tonight. Then he left.

Mrs. Trevanna came up with a bowl of old-fashioned gruel that Lucinda had never eaten in her life before, but which she had to admit was soothing after her recent experience.

She had felt increasingly cold and frightened during the hour she had spent down on that beach with Barry whilst he struggled with the engine that wouldn't start. When the giant wave had so suddenly carried her off her feet, she had even wondered whether it was the end of her life.

Now she looked at Max. They were alone. He offered her a cigarette. She shook her head. She looked extraordinarily pretty, he thought, wrapped though she was in one of Mrs. Trevanna's pink flannel nightdresses with long sleeves, several sizes too big for her. The Cornishwoman had refused to dress her in one of those 'bits of cobweb', as she called Lucinda's own nightgowns. The girl's hair was dry now, curling round her head. Max was pleased to see how well she really looked. She was gloriously brown. But her eyes held no welcome.

"Why are you here, and who told you where to find me?" she demanded.

"Never mind about that," he smiled.

"I do mind." She did not return the smile. "I didn't think a soul knew."

"Someone found out by accident and told me. I'm not going to give that name away."

"Very well. But why have you come, Max?"

"May I sit down?"

She looked at him sullenly, under lowered lashes. He was so big, so powerful-looking, he seemed to fill her tiny bedroom, she thought. Unchecked there came into her mind that thought that had struck her before. The thought that, symbolically, this man from Kenya and the lighthouse were so alike.

She said:

"I'm not prepared to discuss anything with you. I just don't know why you've bothered to come all this way."

"Then I won't sit down," he said with a faint ironic smile. "I'll stand up and talk."

"My head's aching," she said in the same sulky voice. "I want to rest."

"If that's true, I'll go away at once."

He turned to the door but she called him back.

"No, wait. I'm being hypocritical. I feel a bit bruised and dizzy but there's really nothing wrong with me."

He turned.

"Lucinda, I've come down here as a friend. Do let me talk to you."

"You could never possibly be my friend," she said, aggressively.

He walked across the room and stared out of her casement window. It was a magnificent sight. The evening sky was still massed with fantastic clouds, streaked with orange. The sea had been whipped by the gale into huge grey-green waves. He could see them foaming around the base of the lighthouse. Lucinda had certainly chosen a wild and picturesque spot for her self-imposed exile. He turned back to her.

"Why did you run away and tell nobody where to find you?"

She lifted her chin.

"If you insist on probing into my private affairs, all I can tell you is that after my engagement to your brother ended, I decided that I wanted to get away and try to sort myself out. I felt sick and tired of the whole lot of you. I *had* to get away, *and* stay away."

"I understand that. There have been moments in my own life when I've needed to get away from so-called civilisation. But you've upset a number of people by leaving no address, Lucinda."

"Not you, I hope."

The sneer in her voice hit him. He flinched from it but gave her a cool smile.

"Yes, even I. I've been quite worried because I've felt indirectly to blame for everything."

"Well, your conscience can be at rest. I've completely recovered. I just don't want to talk about my recent engagement to Derek—if that's what you came here to do."

Now Max frowned. This girl had an uncomfortable knack of probing into the raw places. In a way she infuriated him. But during the last few weeks he had been so angry with himself and embittered by Derek's feeble handling of this girl that he had thought of her only with pity. Now the sight of her, sitting up in bed, glowering at him so sulkily with that bandage around her lovely head, had an extraordinary effect upon him. She was no ordinary person—that was certain. She had to be carefully handled. (No wonder young Derek couldn't cope!)

He said:

"Look here, Lucinda, I behaved rashly in forcing the issue when I did. But it's no good our going over the past. What I want you to try and believe is that Derek also knows he acted rashly but he's very sorry for it."

"Why didn't he come down here himself and say so?"

"He knew you wouldn't see him."

"I wouldn't have seen *you*, either," she said with a hard little laugh, "only I happened to be unconscious when you first turned up."

"All right. Let's say I'm here on Derek's behalf."

"I'm not interested. I've finished with Derek."

"You amaze me. You are a girl with great feeling or you wouldn't have been so upset by the break. I should have thought you still had some feeling left for Derry."

"I don't think you understand," said Lucinda. "The very fact that I did *feel* so deeply about him made me find his behaviour quite unpardonable."

"All right—but at least you can give him a chance."

"He had his chance and lost it."

Max stared at Lucinda in silence, astonished. He would not have credited her with being quite so hard. Is this what rejected love and hurt pride could do to a woman? He supposed so. He began to wonder if he had come nearly three hundred miles to St. Ruthen for nothing.

Suddenly he changed the conversation.

"It's extraordinarily beautiful here, you look very well. I suppose you've been enjoying yourself."

"Yes, thank you."

How hostile, how unfriendly she was! He was conscious again of being slapped in the face and he didn't like it. But he wasn't going to show her that he was at all personally upset. He went on:

"Your parents are worried. Don't you think you ought to come home, Lucinda? I can drive you back."

"No, thank you. If you want to know, I had made up my mind to go home tomorrow. I shall do so the day after, as Dr. Polmerrow wishes me to stay 'put' until then."

Max looked at her curiously.

"The young man you were marooned with asked me just now to give you his good wishes for a speedy recovery. He seems very upset."

"It was all my fault. I made him take me out in the boat."

"He seems a nice kid," said Max, and thought he saw the colour glow under Lucinda's tan and her lashes flutter. Was she sentimentally involved? . . . Had she been caught on the rebound by a fair-haired, blue-eyed Cornish lad who was obviously her slave? But Max could get no more information from Lucinda, for she said:

"My head really is bad now. Please go, Max. And *please* go back to London without me. I'll make my own way home."

"Very well," he said.

He turned and walked out of the room, feeling extraordinarily deflated.

He had found a room at The Lamb—the local inn. He went back there to a lonely evening whilst the gale howled and raged, then died down almost as quickly as it had come, leaving a pile of driftwood on the beach as the high seas receded. By nightfall all was calm. The moon came out. The lighthouse shed its powerful beam across the water. There was peace again.

But there was no peace in Max's mind. He felt disturbed

and resentful because that young girl up there in the cottage on the cliff had rejected him so completely. He had genuinely hoped she would believe he wanted to be friends with her.

Barry came into the bar for a glass of ale with some of his fishermen friends. Max kept apart from them but watched and listened as the boy gave a stirring account of the way his boat had let him down and the few bad moments he had had on the beach with 'Miss Lucinda'. It seemed to Max that every time the young Cornishman mentioned that name it was with a kind of radiance in his eye and a proud tilt of the head as though Barry considered it a privilege to have been involved in an accident with *her*. Of course the boy was in love—that was obvious to Max. He wondered again if Lucinda had rushed out of Derek's arms to *this*. As he finished his own beer he thought angrily:

My half-brother is a dim-witted idiot. Why the hell didn't he come down on his own and storm the citadel and win Lucinda back. What's the matter with him?

Max felt nettled and thwarted. It certainly seemed to him that this was a wasted journey. He had gained nothing by it. But he put a call through to Iris Turnbull. Iris seemed both relieved and enchanted to hear from Max that he had found her friend.

"You really think she means to come home now, Max?"

"She says so."

"Shall I tell her mother?"

"No, she seems to resent interference. I should leave it to her."

"And she's all right?"

Max glanced from the corridor in which the telephone was situated in the brightly lit bar in which Barry was laughing amongst his friends.

"She seems perfectly all right," he said drily.

"I've had Derek on the phone, Max—he's dying to see Lucinda again. I think he's terribly sorry for what's happened. I think he'd like to undo it all."

"Well, every time I mention Derek's name to Lucinda, she just shuts me up."

"Max, I think you're wonderful the way you went down there to find Cindy. You've been wonderful all the way along."

Max would not have been human if he had not felt flattered by such warm appreciation—especially coming as it did so quickly after Lucinda's coldness and hostility toward him. Iris was a dear thing, he thought. She hadn't Lucinda's beauty or character, but she was very attractive in her way. What Max called the *gamine* type; slim and small with dark-brown, fringed hair; gay, narrow, chestnut-brown eyes with thick lashes; and a wide laughing mouth. She was what he called a typical 'sweater-girl' who looked well in short, tight skirts and heavy-knit jerseys. She was not as seductive in the feminine sense as Cindy but she had a boyish charm of her own.

She had also made it quite plain at their last meeting that she had taken an enormous fancy to him. A man need not be necessarily conceited in order to know when a girl looks twice in his direction and Iris had certainly looked twice in *his*. Now she was saying with rather touching honesty:

"I wish I were down there. You sound so gloomy. I feel I ought to be holding your hand."

"I can't think of anything more attractive," he said lightly. "When I get back to Town you must hold it."

"Give my love to Cindy," she said, laughing, "and thank goodness she isn't 'missing' any more."

A few minutes after the call ended he had forgotten Iris. He was worrying about Lucinda again and what best to do for Derek. He knew that Iris was right—Derek did genuinely regret his cavalier behaviour. All that '*I forgive you*' stuff had really been fatal to a girl with Cindy's spirit. Max could see that.

He went out for a walk along the cliffs to blow away the cobwebs in his mind but did not succeed. He slept badly that night in the little stone-built pub. When he woke, it was to a brilliant morning—dazzling sunshine after the storm. The coast looked glorious. The sea was deep-purple and blue, still flecked with white after the gale. The air was so fresh that Max could not be surprised that Lucinda had fallen in love with the place and wanted to stay on here. Despite her unmerciful snubbing, he felt he must see and talk to her again. If he could just be assured that she didn't hate him and blame him entirely for her broken engagement, he would feel better. After all, he had only flown home from Nairobi at a moment's notice to attend her wedding to Derek. What sort of a holiday was he going to have now? He had nothing he really wanted to do alone. He was out of tune with Derry, and certainly not anxious to see any more of Vivian Brill-Burrie. In fact he felt like paying a visit to the Ministry of Agriculture and Fisheries as soon as he returned to Town asking if they would send him back to East Africa at once. He had always felt that women could play the devil with men when they wanted to. His experiences since he had come home hadn't changed his opinion. Before he left The Lamb that morning to walk to the coastguard's cottage and visit the invalid, Derek telephoned.

"Iris has told me where you are. I made her tell me. Thank God you've found Lucinda. I'm in a ghastly state, Max. You've got to help me," Derek blurted out the words.

"If you mean you want me to plead with Lucinda for you, I don't think it's going to work."

"Why not?"

"She won't discuss you. She doesn't want to see me, either. I shall probably drive back later on in the day—I'll drive through the night and get back in the early hours."

"Oh, hell," came Derek's dismal voice. "I *must* see Lucinda again. The whole thing's got right out of proportion."

"I suppose it's flattering for you, my dear Derry, that she's taken it so badly," said Max.

"I never thought she'd be so spiteful."

"People with pride don't like to be *forgiven*," was Max's comment.

"But, dammit, that was only my first reaction. Surely she realises that I have regretted it ever since. Won't you try and make her believe that?"

"I'll try," said Max after a pause.

"She hasn't met somebody down there——?" began Derek in a worried voice, but the operator interrupted him before Max could reply.

"Your time is up. Will you have another three minutes?"

Derek was in a call-box. He went on, miserably:

"I haven't any more change. Do what you can for me, for God's sake. Goodbye now, Max."

Max thought over what Derek had been about to infer as he walked along the cliff. *Had* Lucinda already transferred her affections? *Had she?*

When he reached the cottage, Mrs. Trevanna gave him the good news that Miss Lucinda was considerably better and talked of getting up later on.

"I expect you'd like to see her, sir——"

"Thanks, I would," said Max, relieved that at least Lucinda hadn't given orders that he was to be turned away.

"Young Barry's up there with her at the moment," said Mrs. Trevanna.

Max stiffened.

"Then I'll come back . . ." he began but at that moment he heard a door shut. The young lighthouse-keeper came down the stairs. He had a look on his face which caused Max some uneasiness. A beatific sort of look. He was flushed and bright-eyed and looked very pleased with himself. And as he saw Max he broke out:

"It's a mercy she's all right. I'd never have forgiven myself. She's a proper *angel* . . ."

"You'm lucky things weren't worse, young Barry," put in Mrs. Trevanna, "or you might both be angels now."

Barry laughed and ran his fingers through his thick fair

hair. Max did not smile. The boy was so obviously besotted with Lucinda. How long had he been up there? She obviously did not feel hostile toward *him*. Poor old Derek! And yet, Max thought with some irony, how much sympathy could one really feel for Derry?

Lucinda, propped up against three pillows, heard Max's voice outside her door and shot a quick resentful look toward it. So Max was still around!

She had a sneaking desire to talk to him on more friendly terms and hear all about Derry, Mummy and Daddy and Iris; all of them in Putney. She was sure he must have seen them. But she could still not quite forgive him for what he had done to her. She said:

"Please go away, Max. As I said last night—leave me alone to manage my own affairs."

"Oh, very well—if you insist on being so unfriendly."

"I don't want to see you or Derek," she called out rebelliously, her cheeks red.

"Then I'll push off back to London. I can see I've wasted my time."

"I'm afraid you have," she agreed.

A moment's pause. Then Lucinda suddenly felt ungracious, and ungrateful. It was not really in her nature to be either of those things. And he *had* come a long way. Why? Just to plead Derek's cause? It was really rather good of Max. And it could not but make her feel slightly mollified to know that Derek so bitterly regretted what he had done. *Could* she ever forgive him? She thought of him—so like Barry to look at, only not as simple and much more cultured. She thought with a tinge of real regret of *Mr. Moses*, the dear old veteran car, the good times she had had with Derek; all the plans they had made to live together in love and happiness. It was really awful to think that such a bomb had fallen, exploding all their hopes and wrecking their dearest dreams.

For the first time for three weeks Lucinda felt a strong desire to get home and begin the old life again—to face up

again to the old problems (or new ones)—whichever they
might be. The brilliant sunshine this morning was symbolic.
The storm of her own life had abated. Somewhere, somehow,
there must be some sunshine waiting for *her*.

Suddenly she called out:

"Max."

There was no answer.

She got out of bed, put on her dressing-gown and opened
the door. She felt a little giddy but much better than last
night. By tomorrow she would be herself again.

"Max, are you still down there?" she called out.

But Mrs. Trevanna looked up the staircase and answered:
"Ee'm gone, me dear. Shall I run after 'em for 'ee?"

"No," said Lucinda. "No, it doesn't matter."

"'Ee said to tell 'ee goodbye. 'Ee's off, driving back to
Lunnon."

Suddenly Lucinda felt quite ridiculously sorry that she had
been so unpleasant to Max. Once or twice when she woke in
the night she had remembered coming back to consciousness
to find herself in his arms, being carried through the storm.
Max, the lighthouse, the shield against a buffeting wind. He
had a strange fascination. She could not deny it. She seemed
to hang suspended between her hatred of him and that sensation of being drawn to him as though by an invisible magnet.

She called out, breathlessly:

"Mrs. Trevanna, if you can make him hear you, tell him to
come back . . . after all, there's something I want to say . . ."

"You go back to bed, my li'l dear. Don't 'ee catch cold or
doctor will be on at me," the woman said.

But Lucinda could not go back to bed. She was feeling
stronger and better with every passing moment. Her injury
had been slight. She was young and physically fit. She was
not going to be treated like a frail woman. Quickly she pulled
on a pair of slacks and a thick-knit jersey and walked downstairs. She found Max already in the sitting-room, filling the
room with his presence; dressed as she had never seen him

before, in red Breton canvas trousers, like the fishermen wore; with a white sweater; a silk handkerchief knotted around his neck. She had to admit he looked quite fantastically handsome and quite fantastically *un*like Derek. He said in a stiff voice:

"I thought you didn't want to see me."

"I didn't," she said, flushing, "but I thought it seemed very ungrateful. After all, I'm sure you came down with the best of intentions and it was a long run."

He put his tongue in his cheek. Mrs. Trevanna had retired into the kitchen, shut the door and left them alone. He said:

"One can't enjoy motoring on these roads in September but it's been worthwhile seeing this part of the coast. I've never been here before."

She nodded, embarrassed and rather stupid.

"Yes, it's marvellous."

"Wonderful lighthouse."

"Wonderful," she nodded.

"Oughtn't you to sit down? You look a bit off-colour."

"I'm fine, thanks." But she sat down on the old-fashioned plush-covered sofa with its crochet antimacassars. Mrs. Trevanna's little sitting-room was full of photographs, sea-shells of every size, and china souvenirs from other Cornish watering-places. A canary sang loudly in a cage beside an aspidistra in the window. Max, she noticed, was so tall that his head almost hit the beam above him.

"Let's relax and talk sensibly," she said in a low voice.

"That's all I came to do but you seemed so anti-me and Derek and the whole lot of us."

"I'm sorry," she said, accepting the cigarette he offered, "but I've been through rather a difficult time."

"I think we all have . . . I know I could kick myself a dozen times over for ever opening my big mouth."

"That was my first feeling but my second is that I'm glad you did," she said, puffing at her cigarette. "I don't think it would have done for Derek to have married me and then had dear Vivian opening his eyes to the horrible truth about me."

Max gave her a quick look, then away again.

"Hasn't it all been rather exaggerated, Lucinda?"

"You mean on Vivan's part? Yes, I told you that long ago but none of you believed me. And as Wilfred Brill-Burrie is the only person who can back me up, and nobody knows where he is, it can never be proved, can it?"

"I don't think Derry wants proof any more," began Max, dutifully. But she interrupted him.

"Don't please start pleading for Derek."

"Very well," said Max abruptly. "I admit he ought to say these things to you himself. Maybe when you get back to Town you'll give him a chance."

"I don't know. I still feel very mixed up. I really want to be free—yes, that's what it is. I want to feel free until I've thoroughly sorted myself out."

Now he gave her a fleeting smile and she saw how charming he could be when he looked at a woman that way.

"Haven't you done some sorting out down here amongst the seagulls?" he asked with humour.

She gave him the ghost of a smile in return.

"I've had a try. But I'm not absolutely clear in my mind as to my future."

He thought of Barry.

"You don't by any chance want to stay down in St. Ruthen for any special reason?"

To his surprise she answered without hesitating:

"Definitely not. I want to get back to my own home and my own job. I owe it to Mummy and Daddy—and to my employers. They've been very patient with me."

Max thought: *Then perhaps it isn't Barry, after all. Perhaps she's just fed up with men in general. I don't blame her.*

Suddenly he leaned forward and said:

"Would you accept my word if I tell you that *I* myself don't care a damn whether Wilfred Brill-Burrie turns up and whitewashes your reputation—or blackens it. I believe in you, Lucinda, and I'm damned angry with Vivian Brill-Burrie for ever starting this damnable business. I can see it's all been out of pure spite."

Her heart leapt with sudden warmth. If he really meant this, she could be glad. If he really wanted to be a friend, what woman would reject such a friendship? (Or such a man.) Her cheeks turned pink and hot:

"Thank you, Max," she said.

Now they looked at each other for the first time without rancour. She began to question him about her parents and friends—those he had been seeing lately. He talked enthusiastically of Iris. And he kept bringing up Derek's name. He was trying to excuse Derek. She knew he was being loyal but found it vaguely irritating. She was also intrigued to discover that he and Iris had become friendly. She knew Iris so well. She was a girl who formed sudden attachments and felt intensely about them. Had Iris fallen in love with Derek's handsome, masterful brother from Nairobi? Things certainly never stood still, thought Lucinda. When she got home, she might find life very different—in many ways. She couldn't wait to talk to Iris about Max. As for Derek—vaguely she wished that Max would not keep begging her to see him. She wished, too, that Max had come down here out of a personal desire to see her, not only because he wanted to be Derek's ambassador.

They went on talking in a friendly way. Mrs. Trevanna brought them coffee. Before Max left again, Lucinda found herself in a state of slight confusion about her emotional reactions to Max. But she had at least rescinded her original refusal to let him drive her home. He had convinced her that it would be silly of her to waste the money on the fare, when she could take her place in his car. He was quite willing, he said, to stay on at The Lamb until she was fit to make the journey.

12

THE drive back from St. Ruthen to London with Max was something of a revelation to Lucinda.

They set out from Cornwall soon after seven a.m.

On that golden September morning when sea and sky looked their most beautiful, it was not easy for Lucinda to bid farewell to Cornwall—to the lighthouse that had been such a symbol of strength and hope to her—even to young Barry who had been her good friend.

Poor Barry had seemed genuinely sad to say goodbye before going back to the lighthouse to look out on those swirling waters and attend to his lamps. She would often think of him like that, and as the good companion of her exile. Even the adventure in the motor-boat which had ended so badly, she would remember as something *different*. And after all, wasn't that what one needed in life, she asked herself; just something out of the ordinary to add spice to an existence which was apt to become dull and monotonous—not only for her but for the average person.

Then she drove beside Max (that other lighthouse, as she called him) back to London. She was astonished, as usual, to find how little he had in common with his half-brother. He did not even share Derek's love of cars nor his knowledge of them. *Mr. Moses* would have bored him. Max drove fast but carefully and with no interest in the engine.

"And I'm not the only one," he remarked. "There are very few drivers who'd know what to do if they broke down, so let's hope we get through in this hired object without trouble."

That made her smile. He was so much less careful and meticulous than Derek; although one thing the half-brothers did share was their rather old-fashioned courtesy. Derek had never been anything but attentive in all the little ways that matter to a woman; the door opened for her . . . the cushion at her back . . . the enquiry as to whether she felt in need of a rest or wished to cover a few more miles.

Max gave her an excellent lunch en route and now she began to learn so much more about him as an individual—his absorption with wild animals, his grief at the neglect, the torture and death to which they were being subjected, both by ignorant natives and through the drought.

He seemed never to have lived a conventional life—he dreaded settling down to a nine-to-five job, with week-ends behind a mowing-machine or staring at TV. And when Lucinda, who had quite forgotten her antagonism and found that she was growing interested in him, and impressed, reminded him that that was surely the fate of millions, he gave her a quick smile and replied:

"Then I shall refuse to become one of millions."

"Won't you ever marry and settle down, then, Max?" she asked.

"One day, perhaps, but I think my wife will have to put up with wandering. No woman will ever cure my love of adventure and exploring."

Very, very unlike Derek—who loved his quiet job as a biochemist, she reflected; his orderly life. Yet once she had loved him and wanted to be his wife. A girl tied to Max would have a hard time but certainly her life would not lack excitement. Lucinda's own sojourn in St. Ruthen taught her, like Max, to enjoy solitude—being segregated from the workaday world. And she, too, had needed the thrill of adventure when she was very young. Wasn't it that part of her nature which had led her into difficulties?

By the time they reached Town, she felt she had got to know Derek's brother quite well. They talked and laughed incessantly. Neither of them referred to the past. They might have been two very old friends. It was strange, she thought. When they pulled up outside her home and she thanked him for driving her, she said:

"Won't you come in and see my parents?"

He looked down at her, his hand on the door of the car. He, too, had found the long drive a friendly, entertaining affair. Lucinda was quite changed—quite, quite charming. She looked radiant and none the worse for her accident. Only a piece of adhesive plaster on the temple to show for it. He said:

"I won't come in, thanks. I phoned Derek last night and we're meeting at my hotel for dinner."

Lucinda nodded. Rather awkwardly, Max added:

"May I tell him that you'll see him if he comes here?"

"I s-suppose so," she said in a halting voice.

"Please do. I think the boy's genuinely remorseful."

"Oh, very well," said Lucinda, feeling awkward.

"I'm going to try and get back to a job in Kenya as soon as I can," went on Max.

She felt a peculiar dismay—almost a sense of panic as though she dreaded losing contact with this strong, compelling man. She stammered:

"P-perhaps you'll c-come and see me again, yourself, tomorrow."

"Thanks," he said. "But I have a date with Iris. I'm taking her out to dinner. We could perhaps both come in for a drink with you and your people. I've never liked the situation and I'd be glad to feel that they did not now regard me as the 'nigger in the woodpile'. Especially now that I've brought you home," he added with that quick smile which she found so extraordinarily attractive.

He was a man, she thought, of strong inner convictions, quiet resolve—a man who walked alone and might be led but never driven. The type who could not show his innermost feelings easily, and who would soon put up an invisible barrier. Yet that barrier was immediately broken when he gave that warm, understanding smile. Confused by her own change of attitude and feeling toward him, Lucinda said good-bye but not before she also experienced a feminine envy of Iris whom he was going to take out to dinner tomorrow. She could not wait to talk to Iris about Max—the man who had arrived only a few weeks ago from East Africa and made such an impact on all their lives.

Now she gave herself up to the reunion with her parents. They were so thrilled to have her back and gave her such a warm welcome that she felt slightly ashamed for having run away and worried them so badly. But before the evening ended, she was quite forgiven. Mr. and Mrs. Mace were truly glad to see her looking so brown and so fit. They listened breathlessly to her account of the storm, being caught by the tide and hauled up the cliff; and Mrs. Mace was particularly interested by what Lucinda had to say about Max. She said:

"I think he was grand to drive down and fetch you back. He's certainly turned out to be a man with a conscience. Daddy and I take a much better view of him than we do of *Derek*."

Lucinda hurriedly and with generosity tried to defend her ex-fiancé.

"I think things got Derek down to such an extent that he did not know where he was or what he was saying. He's trying hard to get me back now."

"But you'll never renew your engagement, *surely*!" exclaimed her mother.

"I don't know. I can't imagine it," sighed Lucinda.

"Personally I think *Max* is the better man," remarked Mr. Mace.

Now Lucinda went scarlet, then laughed as though at a good joke.

"There's certainly no question of anything like *that* with Max and me. To begin with, he's a born bachelor and going back to Kenya, and I don't suppose we'll ever see him again."

"Oh, I think he finds you very attractive, dear," said Mrs. Mace with a typical mother's rosy outlook.

"Oh, no. Don't forget that I was the girl with a bad reputation who stole a married man from his wife. Nobody's yet proved that I'm *not*."

"Of course that was utter nonsense and I think we've all convinced Max of that," remarked Mr. Mace with a touch of his usual pomposity.

"I wouldn't be too sure," said Lucinda in a low voice.

And that was precisely what she repeated to her friend Iris when they met the following morning.

The first person Cindy telephoned was Iris who came rushing round to see her. After the preliminary hug and kiss, the two friends settled down to a cup of coffee and one of their old 'gossips', but with a difference, Lucinda thought wryly; for if Iris found her a bit changed by recent events, she found Iris very much so. Usually so quiet and often lacking in self-confidence, Iris seemed to be on top of the world. Today she literally bubbled over. And of course Max was behind it. The name *Max* was frequently on her lips. He was gorgeous—he was the most sympathetic, the most delightful, the most *real* man she had ever met. She had seen him several times while Cindy was away, and completely 'fallen' for him. She was longing for her dinner with him tonight.

Lucinda felt suddenly years older and wiser than her friend. It seemed so long ago (although it was no time at all) that *she* had been starry-eyed like Iris—all alight with the wonder and magic of being in love. For Iris did not dissemble. She openly admitted that she was in love with Max Chalmerson.

"Surely you can understand why—even if you dislike him for what he did to you in the first place. He did it for the best, darling. You'll grant me that."

"Yes," said Lucinda, "I'm sure he did and I don't actually dislike him any more."

"I think he wants it all to blow over and for you and Derek to come together again. Do you think you ever could?"

"I *can't* think—I'm too uncertain of myself and of Derek—and of everything."

Iris looked at her best-loved friend with concern.

"Oh, Cindy, don't let it get you down. You've had time to wash it all out of your hair, haven't you, sweetie?"

"I honestly don't know, Iris. I'm just going back to work tomorrow and I don't want to be involved in anything—with anybody."

"Well, I'm involved," laughed Iris. "I know Max means to go back to Kenya and he may be the non-marrying kind but I just dote on him, and I thinks he likes me. He's cut all my boy friends right out. They all seem wishy-washy and *ordinary* after Max. He really is so different—isn't he?"

Lucinda had a sudden vision of Max sitting at the wheel of the car with a cigarette at his lips, driving her through the West Country; stopping to give her a meal and a drink; fascinating her with all those wonderful stories of his of the animals in the Game Reserve; his own varied experiences. And again she remembered the moment when she had opened her eyes during that awful storm to find him carrying her in his arms through the wind and the rain.

"Yes, he is different," at length she nodded. "I'm glad you've made such headway, darling. I hope you'll have a wonderful time tonight."

"And I hope things will come right for you with Derek again," Iris said breathlessly.

That night Derek came to see Lucinda.

Deep down inside she knew that she did not really want him, yet she had half promised Max that she would see him, so she did. She almost wondered whether it was only *because* of Max. Once she had vowed never again to speak to the man who had hurt her and let her down so completely, in matters of love and faith.

Max and Iris had just come in for their glass of sherry before going off to their dinner. Max—very gay and obviously ready for a 'party', and Iris, looking very pretty and blissful. It really looked to Cindy as though Iris might possibly make Max change his ideas about bachelorhood. Lucinda felt lonely and even dejected after they had gone. Then Derek arrived.

Funny she thought, how completely he had gone out of her life and her thoughts down there in Cornwall. It was as though she had never been part of his life or he hers—a close part, too. As though she had never been on the verge of marrying him—never thrilled to the touch of his lips or the sound of his voice.

It was an embarrassing meeting. Derek was flushed and his gaze wavered before hers. He seemed thoroughly ill at ease. She did not know *what* she felt, herself. Odd, to say the least of it. He might have been a stranger walking in and yet he was the same old Derek—very good-looking with his slim upright figure, his fair complexion, his boyish smile and the gentle voice and manner that had first attracted her (oh, so unlike his big overwhelmingly powerful half-brother who seemed completely out of place in London, in any quiet conventional society).

But Derek's blue eyes were so unhappy that the soft side of Lucinda's nature asserted itself. Impulsively she held out her hand:

"Derry——!"

"Oh, Cindy," he stammered, and caught the hand and kissed it, which was a thing he had rarely if ever done before. He had never been the Continental hand-kissing type of lover. Then he tried to take her in his arms.

"Cindy, I'm damnably sorry. I couldn't be more so. I was a fool, darling. An absolute idiot, to behave as I did. I was rather taken aback when that ruddy woman, Mrs. Brill-Burrie, first spilled that story about you. I oughtn't to have listened. Only to you."

Lucinda pulled away from him. Funny how cool, how apathetic she felt and how hard it was to conjure up any of the old passion for him.

She said in a low voice:

"Something of what Vivian said *was* true."

"But not the part that mattered. I saw her once or twice when you were away. I soon got fed up and suspicious of her rather than of you."

A bit late, Lucinda thought ironically. *It's a man's first reactions to what he hears that matter, not the afterthought.*

Derek went on to mutter excuse after excuse. Certainly he managed to convince Lucinda that he regretted the way in which he had originally behaved and that he wanted desperately to be forgiven. There was no question now of Derek being the one to forgive Lucinda.

"Take me back, darling," he said huskily. "Give me a chance. Honestly I've been through hell. It was awful when you disappeared like that. I couldn't be more grateful to Max than I am for what he's done. He's damned sorry about it all, too, you know."

Lucinda nodded, but her eyes turned away from Derek. He could not read her thoughts. How marvellous she looked, he thought—with that wonderful tan—that new touch of dignity, of maturity. He tumbled headlong into love with her again.

"Please, Lucinda, let me put the ring back on your finger— our little ring——" He began to hunt in his pocket but she stopped him.

"No, Derek, please, I couldn't take it . . ."

He looked agonised.

"Won't you even give me the chance to show you I regret ever having doubted you?"

"I . . . I just don't want to be engaged again."

"Never? You mean you'll *never* take me back?"

He turned quite pale.

The tears suddenly filled her eyes. She wanted to cry and could not (or would not). She felt physically well but emotionally sick and bewildered. She thought of Max and Iris dining together. She thought of her growing admiration for *him*, rather than of her lost love for Derek. She was torn in two. Yet Derek seemed so sincerely, genuinely anxious to prove that all would be well again if she would give him the opportunity. Her old feelings would revive for him he said, he *knew they would.*

"*Mr. Moses* has been desolate without you. I've hardly been out in the old car at all as you weren't here to go with me. Let's take *Mr. Moses* down to Brighton on Sunday. Oh, please, Cindy, don't punish me any more!"

The thought of the Veteran *Mr. Moses* roused her tenderness, but she could not accept the ring that Derek kept trying to press into her hand.

"No. No engagement—but we'll go on seeing each other if you like, and being friends," she said painfully. "We'll see how things work out but let's give it time."

He seized her hand.

"Oh, Cindy," he said, emotionally, "I'll *make* you love me again. I swear I will. I won't ask you to be engaged again, say for three months. Until Christmas."

"We'll see, Derek."

And that was all that she would say to him. All she *could* say.

They'd give it till Christmas. Then she'd see . . .

13

ONE cold, wet Saturday morning about a week before Christmas, Lucinda left home to go on a shopping expedition. Ruchelle's was open but the girls took it in turn to have a Saturday morning off—part of the bait with which Madame Colette lured her girls to stay in the establishment.

This was Lucinda's day off. She could not have had a worse morning. The driving rain was fast turning to sleet and there looked no chance of its being a white Christmas. Only this bitter, unpleasant sort of weather.

Lucinda shivered although she was wearing a warm coat with a woolly hood over her charming head, and a nylon waterproof. When she left home, it was with a shopping basket and a long list that Mummy had given her, and she had also decided to buy her own Christmas presents. She knew she'd left it late but she hadn't had the heart lately to go on a shopping spree. Christmas used once to be a gay, happy season for her. But this year things were different. So much had happened—so much, in particular, since Max came.

It seemed more like three years than four months to her since that fatal night of her engagement party when Vivian had recognised her and everything had changed.

What sort of Christmas would it be now? Mummy wasn't very well. Daddy was certainly doing much better on the Stock Market again and the finances had improved considerably. But home wasn't what it used to be. There was a shadow over it. That shadow, Lucinda knew, was mostly of her own making. Only last night when Mummy came into her room to bring her hot milk and say good-night (which she still did—just as she used to when Cindy was a small girl) she had said:

"What's on your mind, darling? You're *so* thin! You just

don't seem to put on weight. And it isn't because you're having to diet. Your figure was marvellous as it was. You aren't at all the girl you used to be and after all——"

"And after all, my troubles are over——" Lucinda had broken in. "Vivian Brill-Burrie has left London and gone abroad. Derek keeps apologising for ever having doubted me, and I could marry him tomorrow if I wanted. Guy has left the flat and Max has moved in with Derek and is very friendly toward me, so everything in the garden is lovely, or seems so, doesn't it?"

Mrs. Mace had looked sadly at her daughter.

"It isn't like you to be sarcastic, darling."

"Like you've just said—I'm not the girl I used to be," Lucinda answered, sombrely.

"Don't you think you could ever forgive Derek?"

Cindy's head had shot up.

"Would you really like me to? Do you and Daddy still fancy Derek as a son-in-law?"

Mrs. Mace who had always been rather pacific, and feeble in her efforts to face the solid facts of life, had sighed:

"I don't know, dear. He's a nice boy. He didn't come up to scratch in the summer but he's shown how sorry he is since. Have you lost all your old affection for him?"

"Oh, Mummy, I'm too tired to discuss it—just let me go to sleep," Lucinda had cried and turned over on her side. So her mother had apologised gently and gone out of the room.

This morning Lucinda was sorry because she felt she'd upset Mummy and inadvertently snubbed her. But even her beloved mother could not be allowed to probe too deeply into Lucinda's heart. Lucinda, herself, hardly dared dig down because she knew what she would find. The terrible (yes, it could only be called terrible in the circumstances) truth was: *she had fallen in love with Max.*

It was such a shattering thought that it played havoc with Lucinda's nerves. Perhaps that was why she was so thin, she thought, and nothing seemed bright or beautiful any more. Even the fact that she was doing well at Ruchelle, was head vendeuse and earning a jolly good salary, and had made quite a number of new friends in Putney, and could go to as many parties as she wanted, did not cheer her up. She was bored by the parties and by the young men she met. Derek telephoned every day and came to see her whenever she allowed him to. But she found him as boring these days as her new acquaintances. There was nothing in Derek that reminded her of the young man she had once loved so deeply. That love had literally been torn out of the depths of her heart by his own actions. Now it was lost and she could not find it again although she hadn't so far openly told Derek so. She was giving him the three months' trial—as he had requested.

He was being generous—against her wishes he sent her flowers regularly. When they were out he tried to buy her presents which she wouldn't accept—just as she refused to take back the engagement ring.

They went out in *Mr. Moses* together. Sometimes they got back on to the old friendly basis and laughed and joked together. They enjoyed some of these outings. He took her to one or two good plays and films. He was her partner at a local dance. But whenever he tried to make love to her she felt the same dead feeling—a hopeless sort of feeling which haunted her. It was so awful to feel so indifferent toward someone you'd once loved.

"You're terribly hard and unforgiving—I can't understand you," he had told her sadly the other night when she refused to kiss him.

She had looked up into his nice, boyish, sulky face and sighed deeply. If he only knew how much she wished she *could* feel her former desire, the old responsive glow he used to wake in her. But all she could do was to give him a sisterly peck on both cheeks and try to laugh the matter off, then feel guilty because she knew she had hurt him—he looked so forlorn.

She just didn't love Derek any more. It wasn't that she was hard or unforgiving. She really *had* forgiven him for his attitude toward her—his suspicions. But the truth was she no longer cared whether he believed that she had been good— or bad—in the past. A love affair *could* end this way—she had begun to realise that fact. One false move and the glorious bubble of love burst—it was a frightening thought.

"I don't believe it need be so with all loves," she kept telling herself. "There must be another kind that is so enduring and deathless that nothing could ever shake it. Neither Derek nor I could ever have cared enough. Thank goodness we didn't marry. We would have built up our lives on a fragile foundation. I'm sure he's only trying hard to get me back now because I've shown I don't want him. Human nature is so perverse. Some folks always want most the things they cannot get."

Was it like that with her—about Max?

She couldn't get him. Of course, she hadn't tried. She could hardly admit to herself how desperately she loved him. Nor could she decide when that love had first taken root. She only knew that it had come to flower in the most un-fortunate way and that *she* was the one who was going to be hurt and not Max, and she would never dream of letting him know she felt like this.

As she took the bus toward Harrods where most of her shopping was to be done, Lucinda gazed with unseeing eyes through the driving sleet at the Christmas crowds. They crowded the streets but everyone looked miserable. Not much window-gazing on such a wet, grim morning. Seven more days to Christmas! She had already seen the decorations in Regent Street—the terrific colourful display on the façade of Selfridges. The usual annual attempt to turn London into a playground during Christmas. But she heard no answering echo within herself, felt no desire to take part in the festivities.

On Christmas Eve a party was being held at the Turnbulls' house. Iris had, of course, invited Lucinda. And Max would be there. Oh, yes, Max would be there! Lucinda thought with unaccustomed bitterness. He was so often there or Iris was often out with him. Lucinda was quite positive by now that Max had fallen in love with her best friend.

She looked back through the past few months. She hadn't found it easy to take up the threads of her old life again after her return from Cornwall. She began to think more and more frequently about Max and gradually to realise how much more he attracted her as a man than Derry had ever done. Then she had felt positively frightened. She did not want such a thing to happen. It seemed too incredible when she remembered how much she had disliked him and resented his original interference. She half wished he would go back to Kenya. But he had taken the place of the colleague Guy in Derek's flat because Guy had suddenly been transferred to another part of England and Max had decided to stay in London.

From that time onwards Lucinda saw quite a lot of Max. Sometimes with Iris—sometimes with Derek. Nearly always, now, Max appeared at the parties given by Lucinda's circle of friends in Putney. He was absolutely friendly to her—most amiable nowadays. He might have been her best friend and, indeed, might *wish* that she should become his sister-in-law. He behaved as though the past had been completely wiped out. Iris, too, kept saying things like:

"You know, Max really likes you now—he admires you tremendously, darling. He's sorry he ever tried to break things up between you and Derek."

Sorry . . . everybody was always *sorry*, Lucinda thought, rather angrily. Sorry, so much too late! She had nothing to thank either Derek or his half-brother for. Or *had she*? Would she always be grateful that Max had prevented her from marrying Derek?

In a hopeless state of confusion, she went about her old life and worked harder than ever. But after each successive meeting with Max she seemed to feel that strange magnetism pulling her slowly but relentlessly toward him. He, of course, was unconscious of it—she was certain of that. But when she was with him, either alone or amongst others, she always felt the force of his personality. He gave her that sensation of utter security that she had missed with Derek.

His extreme good looks were one thing—but there was the intrinsic worth of the man himself; Max the traveller, the hunter, the would-be saviour of wild animals in Africa.

He had a job back in Kenya lined up for next year. At the moment he was busy with an International Fund with the target of half-a-million a year toward preserving the Big Game. One Sunday he had called to see her before Derek came to take her for a drive. He pulled out a lot of pamphlets and papers and tried to interest her in his work.

"If ever you have any time, Cindy . . ." (he had even taken to calling her by that nickname) "I wish you'd enrol in this and help me. I've had a letter this morning from a colleague of mine in Nairobi. Listen to this and see if it doesn't break your heart——"

They had sat smoking there together in front of the fire. She watched him while he read aloud from an air mail letter.

Some of his rich tan had faded during the winter but he was still brown and lean and immensely vigorous-looking, she thought. He was a man who would never do anything by halves. He gave himself up to this crusade for wild animals— all of himself—and whatever he did it would be this way. She felt quite faint at the time, for her rich imagination betrayed her into the vision of Max in love. *If* Max, the so-called misogynist, ever grew to love a woman it would be with all that tremendous power and feeling. What a lucky woman his wife would be. And then the colour had burned Lucinda's face and she had dragged her thoughts away from Max as a lover back to Max who was reading a paragraph about the dying beasts in Kenya.

" '*For months a great drought has killed hundreds of thousands of head of game and cattle. Now comes the great*

*deluge on the Tana river in our barren Northern Area—
eighteen inches fell in two days. As you know, the river is sixty
miles wide and it is immeasurably distressing to see the famous
elephant population drifting down to the coast as bloated
carcases. Something must be done to help these unhappy
creatures or there will be no more elephants left in the world.' "*

Max finished quoting and got up and began to move up and
down the room. Dreamily, Lucinda watched him. Her
mother's pretty, conventional sitting-room became a prison
and Max with his leonine head, his swift graceful movements,
brought to mind the wild animal pacing up and down, up and
down, in the hopeless quest for freedom. Max didn't want
freedom for himself but for the animals. Freedom, drink, food
and peace. He turned to her and his brilliant gaze rested on
her for a moment, full of pain.

"It really upsets me, Cindy. You remember that coloured
spool I ran off for you and your friends the other night—those
pictures of the elephants bringing their young down to the
river to drink, after sunset. Unless they're attacked or
frightened, they're such gentle creatures. I love them. But
I've seen them just as my pal Jack describes in this letter—
dead, mercifully dead perhaps, after the long torture of
thirst. But oh, the babies with them! We must have money
to deal with this thing, Cindy. Help me with the fund if you
can."

He fired her enthusiasm and roused her pity.

"Of course I'll try and help, Max. I'll start a collection."

"Every shilling will help, my dear."

Before he left, he had thanked her and for a fleeting moment
touched her shoulder as he said farewell.

She had been ashamed of the riot of emotion that light,
friendly touch had suddenly wakened. Her senses, asleep for
so long, had revived, alarmingly. She had gone up to her
room and locked herself in and not dared come out until she
had recovered her sense of humour. But she rapidly lost it

again when Iris telephoned, as she often did nowadays, to say
that she had been invited to drive down to a big boys' pre-
paratory school with Max the next morning. Max had a
friend—the history master—at that school, and he had offered
to show the boys a film of wild animal life in Kenya.

"He wants to take me—won't it be fun? He said he hates
driving around England alone," Iris had said excitedly.

"Great fun for you, darling," Lucinda had answered in a
high, light voice.

She was going to the pictures with Derek tonight. But with
all her heart she wished she were in Iris's shoes. That *she*
was to be his companion and drive down to Cobham with him
and be there when he produced his film for all the excited little
boys.

It would be quite an honour for Iris, because Max was not
unknown in the Big Game world.

All that day Lucinda had found herself wondering whether
the masters and boys would think that pretty, smiling Iris
was Mr. Chalmerson's 'girl friend'. Perhaps she *was*. Perhaps
she *would* pierce through that armour which Max always told
everyone he wore against the slings and arrows of love.

Why shouldn't he fall in love with Iris? That was another
question Lucinda often asked herself. Iris was a charming
person—sweet to look at and talk to, and she was certainly
very keen about him. Amongst the miseries that Lucinda had
to suffer was listening to long effusions from Iris about Max.
How wonderful he was; how handsome; how madly in-
teresting.

There were no two ways about it—Iris, too, had fallen for
Max. Her former boy friend who had escorted her that night
at the Savoy (which now seemed to Lucinda so long, long ago)
had vanished—his nose badly out of joint.

"I'm so thankful Max is staying on in Town and not going
back to Kenya till the New Year, aren't you?" Iris had asked
Lucinda once, who was forced to reply, casually:

"Yes, I am."

Iris had persisted:

"You do like him better now, don't you, darling Cindy? I mean, he doesn't any longer seem your enemy."

"No, of course not."

"How's Derek?"

"He seems fine."

"I'm so pleased everything's going well with him."

Lucinda had not answered that statement. Iris had a maddening way of taking it for granted that she, Lucinda, would eventually marry Derek. But she could no longer look with the least equanimity upon the idea of having Max as her brother-in-law. No, no, her heart kept crying out. She couldn't marry Derek. It was Max whom she wanted with an urgent passion, the power of which she had never thought herself capable. It was a love which bore no comparison with the immature, rather teenage love she used to feel for Derek.

It was a dejected, harassed Lucinda who pushed her way through the crowds in Harrods this December morning. She was buying presents for both the Chalmersons. They were all going to give each other something on Christmas Eve when the Turnbulls were lighting up their big tree. They always celebrated at this time instead of on the twenty-fifth. Mrs. Turnbull was rather a religious woman and preferred to celebrate on the twenty-fourth and to keep Christmas Day as the Holy Day. *That*, she always averred, was what it had originally been meant for.

The Turnbulls had a big double reception room—theirs was a much larger house than the Maces'. The guests were going to dance. Iris had laid in a store of new records. Already the decorations were up. There would be about thirty people.

Lucinda had a new dress—a personal presentation from Monsieur and Madame Colette. She had tried it on to show her mother the other night, and grimaced over those new salt-cellars in her throat and the sharpness of her shoulder-blades. She was beginning to wish she could put on weight, but her state of mind didn't allow it. Mummy thought the dress gorgeous. Black, with a full short skirt and a bodice of transparent black lace sewn with brilliant blue sequins. She had bought bright blue satin shoes especially for it.

Lucinda had let her hair grow this winter. It was swept up on to one side and caught there with a comb which made her look very *chic*. It was most effective. She knew she would have plenty of admirers, apart from Derek. There was one new friend in Putney—a young doctor who never stopped trying to establish 'contact'—who was coming to the Christmas party. Not bad-looking and quite good fun; much better off than any of them because he had a rich titled uncle who was going to leave him all his money. Dr. James Parnell would have been what Lucinda's parents might have called a 'dazzling match'. But James held no more serious attraction for her than the other boy friends. It was awful, she thought, and an awesome thought, that Max—being Max—just wiped them all off the slate. The worst of it was that she dreaded this Christmas Eve party. Nothing had been said either by Max or Iris—but Lucinda had a suspicion that Max might choose this night on which to propose to Iris and so bring things to a head. Well, perhaps it would be better to get things over, Lucinda thought wretchedly. Better to know one way or the other. And after that she would be forced to accustom herself to the thought that Iris was the future Mrs. Max Chalmerson. Doubtless she would make him a charming wife, upon whom he could depend. Lucinda did not swerve in her own devotion to her girlhood friend; but her cup of bitterness seemed to overflow.

When she got home at lunch-time with all her parcels, she realised that the one person for whom she hadn't bought a present was Max. She just couldn't bring herself to choose it. The things she thought he might like were too expensive—the others were not good enough. But she had bought a pipe for Derek—a silver pencil for her father because he had just lost his—and a really beautiful Shetland silk-lined bedjacket for Mummy. She had already bought a present for her kindly godmother and sent it to the South of France where Lady Hordham was spending the winter in order to defeat her bronchitis.

Lucinda found a letter with a St. Ruthen postmark waiting for her. From Barry, of course. He wrote to her faithfully once a week. Rather ungrammatical and badly written letters, but she liked to get them and hear news of Barry and the Trevannas and the little village she had grown to love—and, of course, of the lighthouse. Barry had been promoted a month ago and was on the way to becoming senior engineer.

It was something to know that he remembered her and was faithful, she thought, as she slit the envelope. Then, when she had read the letter, she gave a little sigh and a smile.

Barry was engaged. To a girl Lucinda had never met— Barry described her as a distant cousin who lived at Mouse-hole.

"You'd like her, Miss Lucinda, and I hope you'll meet her one day when you come down to see us, as we're always hoping you'll do. When are you getting married, Miss Lucinda? I'm very happy and I hope you are, too, and me and my future wife whose name is Nancy send you our kindest regards . . ."

Barry and Nancy. A good Cornish name. Lucky Nancy. She'd won a fine, clean, friendly sort of boy for a husband. Lucinda sat down and wrote warm congratulations to the young Cornishman. But she did not answer that question about her own affair. *When was she going to get married?* Never now, perhaps. Things had grown too complicated. It was all so cynical—that she should be so much in love with the one man whom she used to hate.

Now she felt for the second time, her life's happiness was being destroyed—not through him but *because* of him. This time it was nobody's fault but her own. He had certainly never shown the slightest interest in her, except as his half-brother's future wife.

There was another shadow hanging over Lucinda. The three months grace which Derek had given her in which to make up her mind would be over on Christmas Eve. She would be asked to decide definitely . . . she dreaded it . . . she had been so hurt, herself, she did not want to hurt anybody else. With this new feverish love for Max permeating her very being, she *knew* that her answer to Derek must be 'no'.

When she got home her mother had a telephone message for her.

"Derek on the phone, dear, to ask what colour dress you are wearing at the party as he wants to send you a spray."

Cindy's face puckered and looked as though she was about to cry. She was frozen after standing in the bus queue with the cold wind tearing around her silken-clad legs. Shopping had been a frustrating experience—the things she wanted just did not seem to be there. Those that she had bought she was worried about. Everything was worrying her. She broke out:

"Oh, I wish I didn't have to go to the party."

"But why, darling——" began Mrs. Mace, wide-eyed, but the girl brushed past her and up the stairs to her own bedroom.

Angela Mace knew her daughter so well—it was obvious to her that Cindy was 'in one of her states' but she did not know why. She should just make up her mind about Derek quietly and carry on with the work which she always said she enjoyed. Strange girl, she thought with a sigh; an absolute darling, but much too sensitive and always had been.

14

THE Chalmerson brothers went to the Turnbulls's party in Max's car. Both wore dinner-jackets. Derek talked rather a lot and smoked one cigarette after another instead of his usual pipe. He seemed to be in a state of nerves. Max glanced at him with fraternal affection.

"What's biting you, old chap? Aren't you in a party mood?"

"Not particularly," said Derek.

"Worried about anything?"

"You know darn well I am."

Max stared ahead at the busy street. It had been a fine, cold day. Tonight it was frosty but still clear, with a full moon. Max liked this sort of weather better than the muggy, foggy kind. Since living in Kenya, high above sea-level, he found it almost impossible to breathe here in London.

He was reaching the pitch, he told himself, when he had had enough of old England. Sometimes he wondered why he had stayed so long. He supposed there were two reasons. Concerning his own personal feelings he refused to dwell upon them. The other reason was Derry, of course. He supposed he was waiting to see if things would adjust themselves, and if Derek was going to patch things up with Lucinda.

The younger man spoke again:

"I suppose you know Cindy asked me to give her three months to make up her mind whether she wanted to marry me or not? Tonight's the night when I'm popping the question again . . ." he finished with a nervous laugh.

Max remained silent. He felt none too happy. Derek had changed but Lucinda most of all. There was nothing of the dare-devil, mischief-loving girl in *her*. He found her always extraordinarily quiet these days and even aloof when he was with her. She had been amazingly good helping with his Wild Animal Relief Fund. He was grateful.

Looking back on these last two or three months he had to admit there had been quite a bit of interest and amusement in life for him. He supposed that little Iris had occupied quite a slice of his time. She was always charming to him, but the pace was becoming a little too fast. Things were going ahead a bit too far. He had to confess he was rather worried, not only for Derry, but about Lucinda, Iris—*and* himself. They were all like the pieces on a chess-board, he thought, waiting for someone to move them.

"I say, Max," Derek spoke again, "If you get a chance—*if*—do your best for me with Cindy, will you. Tell her . . . I mean . . . leave no room for doubt in her mind that I—that I really *do* miss our old association like hell and want to get her back."

Max frowned.

"I don't think there's much I can say. I think you've got to do it all yourself now."

"Well, what do you think? You've seen her now and then. Do you think she's really forgiven me?"

Max suddenly snapped.

"I don't know, Derry. Don't ask me that sort of question. I'm not prepared to air my views. I'm keeping out of it this time."

"Oh, all right," said Derek, huffily.

When they reached the house in Putney the party had already begun. They were, according to Iris who met them in the hall, the last to come.

"I very nearly barred and bolted the door and made you two sing for your supper, out in the cold, cold night—a nice carol or something," she laughed.

Max smiled at her and smoothed back his hair. He made one of his most graceful speeches about 'how sweet she looked'. Iris felt, as she afterwards told Cindy, as though her bones literally melted and her heart almost stopped beating.

She had wanted so passionately to look lovely for *him*. And it was for him that she had taken such care to look her best tonight. She wore a white fluffy dress with a very short full skirt, which suited her. Her eyes were starry. When Max handed her a parcel and said: "Merry Christmas," she clasped it against her like an excited child.

"Oh, I know what it is——"

"Yes, a copy of *Born Free*, about Elsa the lioness. It will give you a very good idea of what's going on out in Kenya generally. I know the author."

"I shall adore it!" exclaimed Iris.

Max looked around. The big double drawing-room was gaily lighted and decorated. Iris had a genius for arranging flowers. There was one magnificent display on the mantel-piece—scarlet and yellow spiky chrysanthemum blooms with silvered leaves in a crystal vase. Red-berried holly behind all the pictures. Mistletoe hanging from over both doorways, invitingly, tied with huge bows of red cellophane. One or two couples were dancing. And now Max saw Lucinda. Derek had been quick to find her and was already at her side. Iris followed Max's gaze and said in her generous way:

"You may well stare at our Cindy—she really *is* a smash-hit tonight, isn't she, bless her?"

He nodded. He had never seen Lucinda look quite so wonderful. Entrancing was the word, although he had thought lately that she was losing too much weight. That black *bouffante* dress with the scintillating blue sequins on the low bodice, and long tight sleeves, was most effective. It made her waist seem especially small because the black foamy skirt billowed out, giving her almost the look of a ballet dancer. She wore several bracelets and large black pearl earrings; her long slender throat was bare. She was a very sophisticated Lucinda tonight, wearing more make-up than usual. The beautiful red-brown hair was swept up into a shining crown on her head.

She came across the room now and greeted him.

"Hello, Max. Merry Christmas!"

He fumbled in his pocket for a small parcel but she warded it off.

"No present-giving yet—everything to go on the tree."

"Here's mine from Max, then," said Iris. "I haven't opened it."

Derek had followed Lucinda.

"Come and cha-cha. You do it so well."

They walked away, Iris looked after them.

"Do you think Derek is going to pull it off tonight and that they'll get engaged again, Max?" she asked, dreamily.

It was the second time that idea had been put into Max's mind. For the second time he found that he did not want to discuss the possibility.

"I don't know," he said abruptly. "Come and dance."

She looked as she felt—blissful—as he guided her on to the dance-floor. But he found himself watching Lucinda and Derry, and barely listening to Iris's gay chatter. He really didn't know *what* to think about those other two.

For several reasons, he hadn't wanted to come to this party. He was in one of his 'moods'—he felt almost savagely disinclined for a conventional, thoroughly British Christmas party amongst all these very nice people. And he was furious with himself because right down in the bottom of his soul he knew that he did not really *want* Lucinda to marry Derek. It might work out for the boy but would *he* be right for *her*? That was Max's concern. What a juxtaposition of sentiments, he thought wryly. When he first came home, all that he had been worried about was whether the girl was right for *Derek*. What the Hades was the matter with him, Max? He was right off-beat. Time he got back to the rather uncivilised and untrammelled existence he led in Kenya.

He knew, of course, that Iris was fond of him—more than fond. He couldn't be blind to the adoration in her eyes. She was a darling and he liked her better than any of the 'girl friends' in the past. But he was damned if he was going

to let her be hurt. It wasn't the slightest good anyone at home
thinking that he was a marrying man.

For a long time he avoided dancing with Lucinda.

She knew that he was avoiding her and she was stricken.
For her the party had only begun from the moment Max
came into the house. Derek was being madly attentive and so
far danced every dance with her, taking it for granted, she
supposed, that she still belonged to him. She resented that.
And she knew that she was crazily and quite foolishly jealous
because Iris was receiving all the attention from Max. Iris was
utterly pleased with life.

"I love Iris," Lucinda told herself. "She's my dearest
friend. I ought to be glad she's found someone like Max. And
I'm *not*!"

The tree was lit up just before supper. Lucinda had helped
Iris decorate it. It really looked beautiful and 'oohs' of
admiration came from all the guests when Mr. Turnbull
switched on the gaily coloured electric candles. A white-robed
angel with silver wings occupied the place of honour at the
top of the tree. The glossy green leaves had been sprinkled
with silver snow. Shiny, iridescent globes, tinsel stars, orna-
ments of all kinds and dozens of little gifts wrapped up in red
tissue-paper with a silver-and-gold ribbon, made a dazzling
impression. Mrs. Turnbull put a record on the gramophone
now—an old French song, 'Père Noël'. Now Iris and Lucinda
together cut the presents off the boughs and picked up the rest
that had been laid at the foot of the tree. The present-giving
began.

Lucinda's beautiful face gave away absolutely nothing when
she handed Max his particular parcel. As he took it from her
his hand touched hers. Then suddenly all the lights and
flowers and the people's faces became a kaleidoscope that
dazzled her. She heard him say:

"Thanks awfully, my dear . . ." (Always that 'my dear' . . .
from Max). She had gone to so much trouble to choose that
present. She had really wanted to buy him something much

better but it had to be just a tie—although rather a special one —designed by Balmain.

His gift to her was a small bottle of *Je Reviens*. He joked about it as he gave it to her: "I'll come back . . ." And of course she said it was her favourite scent and in future it would continue to be.

When the present-giving was over they all trooped in to supper. Derek in attendance on Lucinda. She felt rather hysterical and kept making silly jokes with him because she was so afraid he would become intense and propose to her. She was trying to put off the difficult moment—trying to make him dance with some of the other girls.

He insisted on standing beside her during supper, but afterwards she danced with James Parnell—the young doctor who was so openly her admirer these days.

"You look stunning tonight," he told her.

"Thanks a lot," said Cindy.

"I've got a couple of days off this week. I wish you'd let me drive you down to Oxford to meet my uncle," he went on.

"Oh, thanks awfully . . . maybe . . . we'll see," said Lucinda vaguely. But James meant nothing in her life. Through her lashes she was watching Max who was laughing and talking to a rather pretty blonde girl—a cousin of Iris's. As usual, thought Lucinda, he dwarfed every other man in the room. He looked quite magnificent. Would he announce tonight that he was going to marry Iris? she wondered. Everything seemed to be going wrong in her life. The whole pattern of her destiny had gone awry. It was confused and quite unacceptable to her.

As the evening went on—one or two guests had already departed—Lucinda, with a sick feeling in the pit of her stomach, thought:

He hasn't once asked me to dance. Surely he will before it all ends—just to be polite.

Derek on several occasions had begun to say something of significance but she had put him off.

"Not now—wait till the party's over . . . please, Derry——"

When the dance with Dr. Parnell was over she made an excuse and slipped into the dining-room alone. It was deserted now. She stood just inside the doorway, looking miserably around her. She felt incredibly lost and lonely. Then she heard Max's voice behind her:

"Isn't it time you danced with me, Lucinda?"

Her heart jerked. She turned and gave him a set smile.

"Yes . . . I suppose it is, Max . . . if you like . . ."

"Cindy——" he began and paused. His eyes crinkled at the corners. His gaze had travelled upwards. Quite unconsciously, he felt sure, she had placed herself under a bunch of mistletoe.

"This is too good to miss," he said lightly.

"What——?" she began, then stopped, confused, for now her own attention was drawn to the mistletoe.

For an instant his gaze held hers. Then he put his arms around her and kissed her on the mouth. She felt her senses reel. Before she could restrain the impulse, she kissed him back. It was no light kiss between them. It was prolonged and passionate. And from him so unexpected, she told herself, that she was shaken to the very foundations.

When he let her go, he saw that she was absolutely white. He was aghast—at himself rather than Lucinda. He shouldn't have done that. But the intoxication of her kiss was something he had never before experienced. It was just the rather sensual emotion of the moment, so he tried to excuse himself. He had had a lot of champagne. It was Christmas Eve. Lucinda looked most alluring. But she, having got a grip on herself, felt the dangerous moment pass. She spoke gaily:

"That's what your Christmas present has done for me. I'm *smothered* in *Je Reviens*—can't you smell it? It's obviously attractive."

He took his cue from her.

"Absolutely. You see what it did to *me*!"

Yes, she thought. You kissed me that way because you

lost your head. I lost mine, too—but for a very different reason, one which I'll never, never, *never* let you know.

He was not finding it too easy to recover his own equilibrium. He had an uncomfortable memory of Derek, begging him to plead on his behalf. *"Leave no room for doubt in her mind that I really do miss our old association."*

Max thought, savagely:

"Am I to be my brother's keeper for ever more?"

Lucinda said, on a high, brittle note:

"I hear a waltz. Iris adores waltzing. Go and find her."

Max forced the next speech.

"Cindy, I don't want to interfere but be kind to Derek tonight—you know what the best Christmas present you can give him would be——"

Yes, she knew! And she could only presume that Max wanted her to marry his half-brother. She was suddenly outraged. How dared he kiss her as he had just done? That kiss had made her completely *his*—had for ever destroyed her peace of mind.

Max blundered again:

"You do mean to marry Derry, don't you?"

She did not answer. She felt wild—scarcely answerable for her actions. She pulled a handkerchief out of her bag and with trembling fingers opened her compact and looked at the lip-rouge which Max had just smeared. She moistened a corner of the handkerchief, wiped the rouge from her chin and then handed him the mirror. Her voice was even more high-pitched and unnatural. She said, laughing:

"Hadn't you better take a look at your own chin before Iris sees you? She knows the colour of my lipstick."

She gave him no time to reply. She ran from the dining-room back to the dancing crowd in the sitting-room. She still felt weak and wild. That kiss that had been such a revelation—if she hadn't known it before she knew now how terribly she loved this man, Max.

My life's in pieces, she thought, *and I don't seem to be able to pick them up and put them together. I'm powerless.*

Derek came across the room.

"Waltz with me."

"You know how bad you are at waltzing," she said, trying to be jocular.

"I couldn't agree more," he replied. "Let's have a drink and then talk."

It's got to come, she thought, *better get it over* . . .

She could see Max looking unusually stern. Despite what she had said, he had not asked Iris to waltz with him. She was dancing with Dr. Parnell. Max was standing beside Mr. Turnbull, talking—a half-glass of champagne in his hand. He did not look in Lucinda's or Derek's direction.

She allowed Derek to lead her into the dining-room but she did not look up at the bunch of mistletoe which had become so important. God knew what it had done to Max, she reflected—bewitched him, somehow. God knew she wanted to forget that delirious kiss. It had meant so much to her and so little to him. Men could kiss and ride away—wasn't that what they said?

Derek caught hold of her hand.

"Cindy, darling, you're looking very odd. You've lost all your colour. Aren't you well?"

"Perfectly, thanks."

"Tired?"

"Perhaps. I think I'll get you to run me home."

"Of course, but I did so want to talk to you first. I did so want to feel that tomorrow, Christmas Day, you and I——" he broke off.

His blue eyes looked strangely embarrassed and youthful, like his flushed face. She looked at him with some tenderness but without love—without desire. She knew that she could never love him again in *that* way.

"Must it be tonight, Derek?"

"I don't want to worry you," he said miserably, "but you did promise that you'd give me my answer tonight."

She nodded and the answer she gave was literally torn out

of her. She did not want to make it because she knew it would hurt him. He wanted to revive her passion for him—their old happy partnership—and it was all over. She said:

"Oh, Derry, darling Derry, please forgive me, but I just don't want to be engaged to you again. I have tried—believe me—I've given it every chance. We've seen a lot of each other. You've been awfully nice to me. You couldn't have been nicer and it isn't that I bear a grudge against you for what you did. That's all forgotten. It's just that I—I don't love you any more and I don't want to get married."

He lost his colour, then it flamed back. He gave an unhappy laugh.

"So that's *that*! I must say you've dashed my hopes pretty thoroughly. You haven't minced words."

"Isn't it better? We said three months."

"I'm willing to give it longer——"

"No, Derry. It wouldn't be fair to you. I know now that I can't marry you for . . . for all kinds of reasons."

He stared down at her. He could not read her thoughts or begin to guess what lay behind her own obvious unhappiness. He said:

"What a b——y fool I've been! I failed you when you needed me and now it's too late—I'll never be given another chance."

She found herself dissolving into tears. She wept for herself as well as for him.

"Everything's gone wrong, Derry. Everything. Oh, I'm so wretched!"

He put an arm around her, without passion—with genuine affection and concern.

"I'm terribly sorry if *you're* so unhappy, darling. It all seems to be so tragic because it need never have happened. It makes me wish to God Max had never come home, and certainly that he'd never met that foul woman, Mrs. Brill-Burrie."

She hid her face in her hands.

"It might have been worse if it had all happened after we were married and I was made to feel my husband didn't believe in me."

"I have complete faith in you *now*—honestly, darling Cindy."

She looked up, her face wet with tears.

"I'm sure you have. I believe you."

"Am I so distasteful to you these days?"

She shook her head. She could not explain . . . she could only dissemble; make a lot of excuses about just not wanting to get married . . . she told him he must find somebody else . . . she thanked him for his efforts to win her again . . . she was so sorry but it was she who was failing him this time. But when he asked why, *why*, she could not reply.

He said:

"I almost hate Max—I know I'm the one to blame but I wish to God he had kept his mouth shut."

"You mustn't think that way. Don't let me come between you and Max. He's so terribly fond of you. He asked me only a few moments ago to . . . to be kind to you . . ." she swallowed and pulled out her compact, and looked at her ruined make-up. "I must go up to Iris's room and put a new face on," she added with a shaky laugh.

"Well, I'm glad Max spoke up for me," Derek said, a trifle bleakly.

"Let's all be friends," Lucinda begged. "Don't let there be any more msunderstandings and difficulties. Please be my friend, Derek."

Suddenly he took her hand and kissed it.

"You know I will. Always."

"Forgive me," she whispered, and turned and walked away. He followed her into the hall and watched her running up the staircase to Iris's bedroom. As he stood there, lighting a cigarette, Max joined him.

"If you're ready, I'd like to push off, Derry."

"I'm quite ready," said Derek, grimly.

"I haven't said good-night to Cindy. Do you know where she is?"

"I do, and you might as well know that she's just turned me down finally and absolutely."

Max felt his pulses jerk unevenly.

"She has? You mean the whole thing's over now?"

Derek nodded.

"Absolutely over. Cindy will never marry me now."

15

On Boxing Day the Maces gave a small supper party.

It was not intended to be anything in the nature of the 'Big Night' such as the Turnbulls had given on Christmas Eve. Only about twelve or fifteen intimate friends were invited. Iris, of course, many of the old Putney circle, and Max and his brother. But Derek sent a polite refusal. Reading between the lines, Lucinda guessed that he had decided to make a clean break away from them all. He had gone up North to stay with friends for a few days.

Lucinda had never held a party more reluctantly. But the invitations had been issued weeks ago and she could find no real excuse for cancelling them. It was her personal feelings that were involved—her feelings about Max. She knew it and was not going to let relatives or friends guess. But she was in a state of complete despair. Nothing now seemed to be going her way.

Materially she was well off. She could make a new life for herself if she chose. Her godmother had written from the South of France to suggest that Lucinda took a job down there. An old friend of Lady Hordham's—the Comtesse de Maligny—had just taken up residence in a wonderful old château in the hills behind Nice. Her young grand-daughter, Sophie, was living with her while Sophie's parents were away on a world tour. It was suggested that Lucinda should stay with the Comtesse for six months or more, if it was a success; and be a companion to Sophie. At the same time she could help the young girl to improve her English.

Lucinda's godmother had offered all kinds of inducements. The glamour of the South of France, the sunshine, unending parties.

In one of her letters she wrote to Lucinda:

"You have had a bad time since that wretched Brill-Burrie
affair. I know you have been unhappy. Now I can assure you
you will have a chance out here to meet some really charming
eligible young men."

Lucinda was grateful but she had no particular wish to meet
'eligible young men'. On the other hand she was positive that
Max would sooner or later ask Iris to marry him. Derek had
gone. It seemed senseless for her to stay in London. Whilst
she prepared for her party, she made a decision to break with
Ruchelle tomorrow and accept this tempting offer from the
Comtesse.

Aunt Mary's letter had finished:

"On no account must you let your young lovely life be
ruined because of that stupid Derek or his misguided brother."

At first Lucinda had laughed over that word *'misguided'*
and then wept. Why must she love the man? Why did the
memory of Max's strong resolute face and the awful, *wonderful*
memory of his kiss under the mistletoe, so relentlessly haunt
her?

Every time she thought about it she built up fresh misery
for herself—the agony of hopeless love for a man who would
never want her.

The last time she would see him would probably be at her
party. Well—one thing was positive—she was not going to let
him find a sad silly girl who was brooding over *him*. She was
not going to give him or anybody else the satisfaction of
knowing what life had done to her.

Whilst helping her parents push the furniture back in the
sitting-room and prepare the cold buffet, Lucinda began to
feel thoroughly on edge. So nervy was she, that she snapped
several times at her mother, vetoed every suggestion that was
made about the preparations, and finally announced that she
'couldn't care less', and left everything to them. She dragged

a lot of dance records out of the cabinet and began to play them, smoking one cigarette after another, singing the choruses.

Angela Mace looked at her daughter. She felt her heart sink. She knew Cindy so well. She knew her in this sort of 'mood'; defiant . . . full of bravado . . . a little reckless, even dangerous. This was a Cindy Mrs. Mace hadn't seen for years. The very young, too-gay Cindy who more often than not used to put on an act like this because inwardly she was upset—or felt insecure.

'Poor Cindy,' the mother thought sadly, 'she hasn't confided in me so I don't really know what's wrong, but *something* is. She can't mind that Derek's gone. It was she who turned him down. And it isn't James Parnell. It *can't* be Max. She's always blamed him at the bottom of her heart for all the trouble.'

"Are you all right, lovey?" she asked the girl after they had sorted out the evening's problems.

Lucinda, having arranged the flowers, was now tying up a piece of mistletoe that had fallen down. She nailed it in a more conspicuous place. A cigarette dangling from her lower lip, she gave her mother a hard bright grin.

"Why shouldn't I be all right, ducks? I'm fine. Sorry I snapped just now. Feeling a bit tired. I'll have an hour on my bed before the party. You must, too, Mummy. I can't have you cracking up again."

"More kisses expected?" asked Mrs. Mace innocently as she watched Lucinda deftly tie the red cellophane bow on the mistletoe.

Lucinda jumped down from the chair on which she had been standing. Her face was crimson.

"What do you mean by that, Mummy?"

"Don't be so touchy, dear," said Mrs. Mace mildly. "I was only trying to be funny."

Lucinda relaxed. Heavens, she thought, why be so unkind to poor darling Mummy? *She* didn't know . . . *she* hadn't seen that kiss in the Turnbulls' dining-room under that other bunch of mistletoe!

Lucinda gave a bright brittle reply.

"Yep, *heaps* more kisses, I hope. I'm going to pep up the party tonight, Mum—I've got a feeling it might be sticky."

And when that party began, she still had that feeling. Dr. Parnell was the first to arrive. He was for the moment her most staunch admirer but he started off by reproaching her.

"I hope you're going to be nicer to me tonight than you were on Christmas Eve. I couldn't think what I'd done. You *did* hand me the frozen mitt, Cindy."

She forced herself to be frivolous.

"Cold hands, warm heart, so don't let *that* worry you, Jimmy."

"Is your heart really warm?" he asked her.

She sighed.

He was nice and, she knew, hers for the asking. Her first instinct was to let him alone but she had made up her mind definitely that she must not let life get on top of her tonight. Not if she died for it. Whatever one lost, it must never be one's pride, she thought. So she looked at James through her lashes and said:

"Absolutely *burning*. Watch out, doctor dear."

"I like danger," he grinned down at her. "And you're looking quite smashing tonight."

She hoped that was true. She wanted to look 'smashing'—to be a smash-hit at her own party—and to let Max (and even Iris) think that she was the maddest, happiest girl in town.

That's what they all used to think she was. The old wildness was coming back. That rebellious feeling that whatever one did people would think the worst, so why not live up to it? Why not show them that she didn't care—that she *was* a Wild One and they could all put up with it.

It was this feverish, unnaturally gay Lucinda who welcomed Max to the party when he and Iris arrived.

Yes, Lucinda thought, of *course* they came *together*, as usual.

Iris wasn't looking her best or brightest tonight. A shade downcast. Perhaps *she* was not going to realise her dream of love after all. Who could tell? Lucinda didn't want Iris to be hurt any more than she liked being hurt herself.

(Oh, damn Max. *Damn him!*)

"My, *my!*" said Max as he looked at Lucinda. "It's like coming into another world after the cold and damp outside. Bright lights here . . . big fire . . . gorgeous flowers . . . and a Christmas Tree still in the window. I shall remember this sort of thing when I'm back in Kenya."

"No doubt we'll all remember you, too," said Lucinda with a burst of laughter that somehow rang false. But she went on laughing. She led Iris and Max into the dining-room where drinks were being dispensed by her father. Champagne tonight.

The guests had all arrived. Max and Iris were the last. A few had started to dance to the tempting music on Lucinda's radiogram. One young couple executed quite a professional cha-cha.

The party had begun.

Iris moved across the room to speak to Mrs. Mace. Max standing beside Lucinda, raised his glass to her.

"Happy Boxing Night, my dear."

"Thanks," she said, then turned and walked away.

She wasn't being friendly—that was obvious to him. But the sight of her stirred him profoundly. If she had looked lovely on Christmas Eve, she looked a hundred per cent more so tonight. It was not only the dress although it was a little startling—one of Ruchelle's most spectacular models—dull gold satin cut on severe, dramatic lines; off the shoulders, mink-edged, with long tight sleeves, and short tight skirt showing those beautiful flowing legs which never failed to stir Max's senses. Her hair was brushed severely to one side into a huge thick wave. Her eyes looked enormous, with more green shadow than usual. But it was her feverish glittering *unusual* look that intrigued and mystified Max. *What was going on,* he wondered.

Now the boy who had been doing the cha-cha, asked Lucinda to dance. Max continued to watch her whilst he smoked and sipped his champagne. He had always thought she had become a rather dignified girl but tonight she was throwing dignity to the wind. She was a marvellous dancer of course. He knew that; but he had never seen Lucinda quite so *abandoned* . . . (yes, that was the word). As though she was throwing inhibitions to the winds. She danced the cha-cha quite madly. And Max could hear her laughter through the music. Everybody else was watching. They all clapped once it was over. One of her girl friends came up to Max.

"Cindy's in good form tonight. I haven't seen her so gay for years."

"She looks curiously *young* . . . rather like an excited school-girl in a sophisticated dress," said Max drily.

Lucinda's friend laughed.

"What a wonderful description! Actually Cindy was at school with me. That's how she used to behave when we first left. She used to make us all die of laughter."

But she didn't make Max 'die of laughter'. This strange hectic Lucinda troubled him more than a little.

Once or twice, he tried to dance with her but she always seemed otherwise engaged. He watched her waltzing cheek to cheek with James Parnell. The way that beautiful body in the gold satin dress seemed to melt seductively into the young doctor's arms, tore a most unusual and unexpected strip of jealousy out of Max's confused mind. He began to wish he hadn't come to this party. During supper she was busy seeing that her guests were served. Finally Max managed to talk to her alone. He forced a plate of turkey and ham into her hands.

"Come on—you haven't eaten a thing, yourself, yet."

"I don't need mortal food," she laughed at him in an impudent way. "I've eaten the bread and honey of the gods and drunk their wine and I feel quite intoxicated."

"I don't recognise you like this, Lucinda," he said quietly.

"Oh, don't you? But of course, you don't really know me," she laughed. "But haven't the others told you how mad I can be?"

Max shut one eye and pursed his lips.

"Aren't you over-acting?"

"*Me* acting?" she asked with simulated surprise. "What do you mean?"

"Never mind," he said crossly.

"Let's hope Derek's enjoying himself," she suddenly changed the subject.

"I rather doubt it. The boy was pretty badly hit when you turned him down," said Max. It was the last thing he really wanted to say but he still felt a tweak of remorse about the boy.

"Oh, don't let's be too sorry for him," said Lucinda. "And stop having a conscience about it, because you know I wasn't the girl for him. Think how shocked he'd be to see me as I am tonight. *You* are shocked . . ." she added with a giggle.

"You make a mistake," began Max, but he got no further. Iris had joined them. Max turned and walked away.

Iris sighed as she looked after him.

"Are you being horrid to him? He looks very depressed."

"My darling Iris—he couldn't care less how *I* treat him. You're the one he wants."

Iris shook her head, her pretty friendly face downcast.

"No, I'm getting wise to myself, I've been a clot, darling. At one time I thought I stood a chance but he did warn me that he wasn't a marrying man. If he'd been going to change his mind he'd have told me so on Christmas Eve. But he didn't."

Lucinda lit a cigarette. Iris could see the slender fingers shaking. Lucinda's mad mood had not passed unnoticed by Iris and now she saw such torment in those wonderful eyes that she puzzled over it. What *had* brought back the old wild Cindy?

"I'm afraid Max's excess of feeling over Derek's happiness originally started the trouble," she said, "but I think he regrets all that now."

"I don't want to talk about him," said Lucinda harshly.

In a psychic moment, Iris suddenly felt as though a shot in the dark had been fired and hit her. She caught her breath.

"Cindy . . . *you* aren't . . . *you* don't feel about Max as I do, surely!"

Lucinda broke in:

"Don't say any more, please. Don't say it, Iris. Just leave me alone."

But it was too late. She had given herself away. Iris, staring after her, *knew* . . .

The evening was drawing to an end. Lucinda's parents had gone to bed and left the young ones to carry on with their dancing. Lucinda determinedly flirted with everybody but Max. Then she suggested a game . . . a game she had been taught by a Swiss girl. One person stood in the middle of the room. Everybody danced around him in a circle. When the music stopped, whoever came face to face had to join forces with the one in the centre. They must kneel down facing each other and exchange a kiss, then dance together. Just a foolish childish game. It was popular when everyone was in party mood like this.

Cindy, on one occasion came face to face with James Parnell, and Max knew a quite ungovernable and most unreasonable rage because for James she had such a gay smile, such a warm embrace.

Then it was his turn. Hardened man, sensible adult though he was, he found himself wishing that the music would stop when he was opposite *her*. He almost hated her tonight. How dared she behave like this? How *dared* she live up to her old reputation?

Somebody stopped the record.

Max had got his wish. He was face to face with Lucinda.

She laughed at him, her eyes brilliant, her face hot, and pressed her hands against his shoulders.

"Down you get on your knees, Oh, Defender of Wild Animals!"

"*You're* the wild one tonight," he said in such a low voice that only she could hear.

"I hope I shock you," she whispered back, and he saw her teeth fasten over her lip, and a curious spark in her eyes met the gleam in his.

They knelt down opposite one another. Max made no bones about the kiss that followed. And she followed the pattern of the evening and kissed him back almost insolently. Everybody cheered. Then she flung back her head, shut her eyes and said in a loud dramatic voice:

"Help me up somebody. I'm about to swoon!"

James Parnell raised her to her feet. The game went on. But Max in a sudden blind rage, walked out of the room . . . and out of the house.

Then Lucinda went from the top of the barometer down to the bottom. But outwardly the laughter and the singing and the dancing went on.

Now I've shown him how little his attitude toward me matters. Now I'll never see him again, she thought.

It was only when the guests had gone, and the house was dark and silent, that she hid her face in her pillow and began to cry bitterly.

16

Now she entered on the last stage of her job at Ruchelle and her life in London.

From time to time, Cindy heard news of Derek. She was not entirely without an affectionate memory of Derek and it had given her quite a pang to hear that he had actually sold *Mr. Moses*.

Iris heard also that he was giving up veteran cars. To Lucinda that seemed, indeed, the end of an era. With the sale of *Mr. Moses* faded the last sentimental memory of the passionate love which the immature, inexperienced Cindy had once given to Derek.

Iris also gave her news of what was happening about Max and herself. They had 'had it out'. Iris had been 'stupid enough', she said, to let him see—probably rather more than usual—that she was too fond of him. She asked him to go to the theatre with her—she had been given two seats by an actress friend—and he refused. Then Iris had said, rather bluntly:

"If you think you are seeing too much of me and giving me ideas, you can count that out. I'm not setting my cap at you, dear Max. I know how you feel. I feel the same."

Whereupon at once he smiled, looked very relieved, and said:

"Good. I'm glad. You're such a sweetie, Iris. I do so value your friendship. But if you don't mind accepting me for the unsatisfactory chap I am—I see no reason why we shouldn't always be pals."

"So I told him," Iris added in a hard, brittle voice, "that was how I wanted things, too, Cindy. No false pride—I just stick to the friendship basis now," Iris went on, her charming face puckered. But her laugh had a sad note to it which upset

Lucinda. As for herself she had not expected to see Max again after her mad behaviour on Boxing Night and he had neither telephoned nor contacted her.

Toward the beginning of February one good piece of news came to cheer Lucinda, even though it in no way filled the void of her own life—or eased the secret anguish in her heart.

Derek—whether on the rebound or out of genuine feeling—had fallen in love again, to Lucinda's secret joy and relief. Max suddenly called to tell her the news, and to see her parents.

Mr. Mace was always pleased to entertain Max. He maintained that he enjoyed an hour with him more than with any young fellow he knew today.

"It's such a treat," Mr. Mace had once said to Lucinda, "not to have to listen to a lot of talk about fast cars or beatnik girls or football pools or, indeed, on any of the unimportant subjects that seem to fill the lives of people today—both young and old. Max is keen on the things that are worthwhile. He carries a torch—has a real purpose in life. One likes to hear his views on Kenya, and the future of the Africas. He's so interested in the political aspect, too, as well as these wild animals—more so than in his own private affairs. He's a very *real* person, that boy."

Max told her that Derek was going to get married to the sister of the school-friend he had recently contacted. Rose Hunston was a good-looking brunette, particularly interested in Derek's profession because she, herself, was a bio-chemist. They were to be married at Easter.

Lucinda, after the first awkward meeting with Max, tried to concentrate on what he was telling her. But she had felt embarrassed and unhappy when she first faced him. He on the other hand, behaved with cool civility at first—then with increasing friendliness—as though he had never walked out of the house that night so abruptly and so obviously disgusted with her, she thought.

"I think he's very happy," said Max.

"So it's all worked out for the best," said Lucinda with a bright, hard smile.

Max frowned.

"Yes, I'm sure it has," he agreed.

And he was satisfied that this time Derek had chosen the right girl. Yet he was not really interested in Rose apart from the fact that she might induce Derry to settle down.

Since the night of the party, Max had been unable to forget the memory of Christmas Eve when he had taken her in his arms and watched the colour of her eyes change, her pupils grow large and dark, her breath quicken, like his own, with desire. He had felt her heart beat crazily against his own— yet, since then, he had tried to believe the moment should not be taken seriously.

But he could not get the fragrance of *Je Reviens* out of his nostrils—still less the remembrance of his senseless jealousy when she had flirted with every man at her own party except himself.

His life's interest lay in his work. Yet the thought of going back to Kenya to take up his new appointment out there, no longer appeared quite so satisfactory. His mind kept turning back to Lucinda. Her sadness, her thinness, the obvious change in her, seemed to him to be all his fault. Yet her crazy behaviour on Boxing Night had sent all the nice ideas he had built up about her recently, toppling.

He thought of her incessantly—till he felt maddened by it. He even found himself picturing her riding across those sunlit plains in Kenya at his side. How wonderful she would look on a horse! He could see her with her head thrown back, her laughing eyes turned to the purple, magnificent mountains, her glorious hair blowing in the warm wind. He could imagine her adoring Kenya and the untrammelled healthy perfect life one could have out there. He began to feel that it was high time he went back to Nairobi and the old bachelor existence. Yet he dreaded going. Never before had Max Chalmerson, who liked to boast that he had such complete command of himself, felt so disturbed—almost as though he were in a kind of vacuum from which he could not escape.

He had just about reached the conclusion that it would be far better if he saw no more of Lucinda. But he was drawn back to her, time and time again.

He spent most of this evening talking, man to man, with Arthur Mace. They discussed the difficulties of the African situation in general—the black domination—British administration and the general effect of world events lately on the country's economy.

"I've got a bit of money in this country. I think I'll have to leave it to you to invest for me, although at one time I had thought of putting it all in Kenya," he told Mr. Mace.

"I certainly shouldn't do that. Wise investments in the big industrial firms over here are the answer."

Max nodded, glanced in Lucinda's direction, and lit the cigar which his host had given him.

Lucinda was sitting on a sofa beside the fire with her mother, who was winding a ball of knitting-wool from a skein which Lucinda held between her hands. The thought leapt through Max's mind:

How lovely she is . . .

Lovely, those slender hands, moving from side to side as her mother wound the wool. Lovely, the firelight, the glow of the lamp on that rich chestnut hair; lovely, the long line of throat, the delicate curve of breast, the long graceful legs revealed by the short skirt that Lucinda wore tonight with a low-necked black sweater. Around that graceful throat there were several rows of huge gold beads. The pleasant jangle of the bracelets on her wrists as she moved her hands fascinated Max.

She turned suddenly and caught his gaze.

For a split second, the man experienced the peculiar sensation that he was falling through space. It was as though some electrical message sparked from those grave and beautiful eyes directly across to his, blinded him and flung him off balance.

He caught his breath, turned back to Lucinda's father and tried to concentrate on what he was saying about the effect of all this trouble with the Colonies, on the Stock Market.

After that, as soon as Max could conveniently leave he went off without accepting the drink Mr. Mace offered.

"I have an appointment at my Club—rather a late one, but I must keep it," he said abruptly.

The Maces accepted this explanation. Only Lucinda, enormously sensitive, guessed otherwise. She, too, had felt the electric shock of that sudden unexpected exchange of glances. But she had misread his, taken it for granted that it was only she, herself, who felt so shattered. That he should get up suddenly and say he must go, was to her just a further sign that he had no particular interest in her; for they had hardly exchanged more than a few words tonight and then it had been on the subject of Derek's new girl friend.

She saw Max to the door and tried to make a few mundane remarks:

"Ugh! It's cold in this hall—freezing tonight."

"Isn't it!" he agreed.

"You'll be glad to be getting back to the warmth of Kenya."

"Sure."

"You said you'd tell me about the trip you're taking down the Tana river when you get to Kenya."

"Yes, I will, next time we meet. By the way, thanks a lot for helping Iris in this Wild Animal campaign. You two girls have been marvellous."

"I've done nothing."

"Thanks all the same," he said abruptly, slipped into his overcoat and tied his scarf around his neck. He did not feel the cold when the front door opened. His whole body seemed to be on fire, which fact both exasperated and puzzled him. No woman in his life before had ever had such an effect upon Max. He almost resented it. His 'good-night' to Lucinda was abrupt. For her it held a chill that was not unlike the cold sweeping in from the ice-bound streets this February night.

It was the chill of death itself—the little death that she must die in her heart, in her mind, when Max went away for ever.

In a bright, brittle voice she said:

"You and I both seem to be shaking off the shackles of this country. I'm off to Grasse at the end of this month."

"Ah, yes, Iris told me. You were to have gone to this friend of your godmother's, Lady Hordham, earlier this month, weren't you?"

"I was, but the Comtesse put me off for a few weeks. Sophie had to have her tonsils out so she is in Brussels and I must wait till she is fit again. I've left Ruchelle's and I'm rather busy with Mummy getting my trousseau together."

Max gave her a quick, gloomy look, then pulled a packet of cigarettes from his pocket and lowered his gaze again, and laughed.

"Trousseau, eh? Sounds like a wedding."

She echoed the laugh derisively.

"Not for *me*, thanking *you*! It's a trousseau for the South of France, where I hope the weather will be warmer and I shall need a few thin dresses."

"Well, good luck, my dear. Good-night."

"Shall we see you before you go?" She tried to appear offhand.

"Yes, of course. I'll look in one day next week and pay my respects to your parents and say farewell," he nodded.

She closed the door on him. For a moment she stood leaning against it, her forehead against her arms, in an agony of mind that she never wished to feel again. It seemed to annihilate her. She felt choked with misery.

"Oh, Max, *Max* . . ." she muttered his name, clenching and unclenching her hands as though the pain was unbearable. In her mind, this was really the end. The end to all hope—all happiness.

17

"I've come to say goodbye to you and to thank you for all you've done for me while I've been in England."

Iris Turnbull looked up at Max with a smile that held a great deal of wistfulness.

They were standing in the dining-room of her home that Saturday afternoon. Iris had just been writing letters. She had also just been writing in the diary which she had kept since she was a little girl. When she thought what she had written this morning, she turned crimson and felt thankful Max would never see it.

"It wasn't his fault that he couldn't fall in love with me. I just wasn't right for him. But having got to know him I think he's such a straight, splendid person as well as an absolute darling. I could have loved him so much. Now I've just got to get over it! I'm not the only woman who has got to get over a disappointment in love. The whole of life seems to be one big lesson. It seems such a pity that one must grow old before one really learns. I believe that Max in his heart of hearts loves . . ."

But Iris had stopped writing at that important point, almost as though she did not want to put into print the name that should be there. Iris had always been a happy sort of girl—cheerful—less emotional, perhaps, less serious-minded than her friend Cindy. She was hard-hit by the fact that she had been unable to make the one man she really loved care for her in return. But she had no intention of letting Max ruin her life. That in her estimation would be too stupid. What really concerned her now was that *Cindy* was so unhappy— much, *much* more so than Iris; which fact Iris had the intelligence to realise.

She had meant to be gay and nonchalant when Max came to say 'goodbye', but did not find it easy. There was anxiety in her eyes as she stood there, back to the fireplace, facing him.

He went on talking on a casual note—thanking her again for the help she had given him in his crusade. She and her friends had done so well, what with their flag days, the Christmas bazaar and the various collections, all in aid of the wretched dying animals in East Africa.

"You've all been terribly good and nice to me personally. I shall miss you and the happy social round in Putney once I'm back amongst the so-called savages," he ended, smiling.

"We shall miss you, Max."

"I must say I'm relieved that I can go away feeling Derry's settled."

Iris made no comment. She had no particular use for Derek Chalmerson. In her opinion, he just wasn't on the same level as his half-brother. She had no use either for the rapidity with which he had swung from his determination to regain Lucinda's affection, to his new love. However—let him marry his Rose and, as Iris had laughed when she discussed the affair with her parents last night, let him spend the rest of his life in a laboratory with her, both of them wearing long white coats, poring over their test-tubes!

Now Max brought up the name that meant so much to Iris.

"I've come here first, then I'm going on to say goodbye to Cindy."

Iris bit her lip.

"There's something I think you ought to know, Max."

She thought he looked suddenly tense and wary but he lit a cigarette and as he put it between his lips, spoke on the same casual tone.

"Fire away. What's on your mind, honey?"

"You remember that the whole trouble with Cindy started through that dreadful woman, Vivian Brill-Burrie?"

"Yes."

"Well, I had a letter from Wilfred, her ex-husband, this morning."

Now Max looked obviously startled.

"You've heard from *him*?"

"Yes. I've always been the sort of girl they write to and confide their troubles in," Iris said with a short laugh, and turned her charming wistful face from Max's searching gaze. "Wilfred Brill-Burrie was quite a friend of mine. He used to practise in this district, you know. I had a slipped disc when I was nineteen after a riding accident and he treated me for a long time. I think he always rather liked me."

"You're a very likeable person, Iris. Just the nicest," commented Max.

She locked her hands tightly behind her back.

"Anyhow, after Wilf went away we all thought we'd seen the last of him. He was so disgusted with life, he never got in touch with anybody in Putney. We only heard about his divorce. Then suddenly this letter arrived from the Cape."

"He is the man who——" began Max.

"Yes," interrupted Iris, firmly. "He is the man who poor Cindy was supposed to have had an affair with, in that hotel in Oversands."

Max began that rather nervous prowling that he liked to do, up and down the room, as though deep in thought.

"Well?" he said.

He wasn't particularly anxious to have the Oversands affair dragged up. Neither was he anxious to say goodbye to Lucinda. He was off to Kenya on Monday but now that the week-end of departure had come, he knew that he was less than ever keen on leaving England at the moment—because of *her*. It was all rather alarming and incomprehensible to him. He didn't like it. Abruptly he said:

"Well, what does this gentleman have to say for himself?"

"You might like to read his letter," said Iris, quietly.

That letter had been on her conscience ever since she had

received it. Of course she had telephoned to Lucinda at once and told her about it. But all *she* had had to say was:

"It's too late now. Tear it up."

But Iris, after thinking things over, had come to the conclusion that it was not at all too late, and she ought, at least, to let Max see what Wilfred had written—even if Derek never now saw it. (Certainly it was too late for Derek!)

Half intrigued, half reluctant, Max scanned the letter that had been written to Iris. The first page told her how Wilfred remembered and appreciated the warm friendship he had once received in the Turnbull household; and that he wanted Iris to know (and everybody else) that he had found contentment and happiness again. For a long time after his divorce he had been so bitter against Vivian, and all that she had done, he had lived entirely for his job as an osteopath. Then he had met a charming woman—a South African widow with two children, living in the Cape, and fallen in love with her. They were now married. He had never been happier in his life. He was learning, Wilfred wrote, what it was to have a really fine wife.

"My Margaret may not have the looks or the devilish fascination that Vivian could put over at times, but she's all that Vivian wasn't. Honest, brave and a fine mother. I have grown to love her children as mine. But I particularly want news of Cindy. That's why I am writing to you, Iris. She has been on my mind all through these years. I can't forget how brutally my ex-wife attacked her reputation. It was of course a put-up job, as we all know. Cindy was a mischievous child but there was no harm in her and for a long time it worried me, thinking that what Vivian did might have had some permanent ill-effect. I would like to hear from you that perhaps life has been kind to her and that she is married now and settled down. Just tell her that I do remember her and still regret that awful night which might so easily have wrecked her life.

"Your sincere friend,

"Wilfred Brill-Burrie."

Max read this part of the letter through to the end. What he felt by the time he came to the last line was indescribable. A mixture of guilt and extreme contrition—above all, the guilt. He should have known, he thought, with a surge of self-loathing, *he should have known*, when he first looked into Lucinda's eyes, that she had been innocent.

He returned the letter to Iris. His cheeks were flushed.

"Thanks for letting me see it. I can't say it's made me feel too good. In fact it's made me quite positive that I'm the biggest so-and-so in creation."

"Oh, Max, why——?"

"Isn't it obvious?" he broke in. "I believed that b——y woman, so I stepped in between Cindy and Derek. It makes me feel so damned ashamed, I don't know . . . I just *don't know*! . . ." he ended. "It doesn't make sense. Look at her on Boxing Night."

"Yes—it was an act. I know Cindy. She was all het up and miserable and she put on a complete act, surely you saw that. You must have realised for a long time that Lucinda wasn't the guilty party in that stupid case."

"I did realise it. I believed in her before Derek ever decided to try his luck again. Brill-Burrie's letter has merely confirmed the fact, but—the other night upset all my calculations. I don't begin to understand her now," said Max gloomily.

Iris was silent. She was no fool and she could see by every word he spoke that Max was in love with Lucinda. Yes—that was the truth—bitter though it was for her to acknowledge. It was then that Iris responded to one of the strongest impulses of her life—a grave, fine impulse which had its roots in her deep friendship for Lucinda. She put herself completely in the background. She said:

"Oh, Max, can't you *see* what's happening?"

"What?"

"She behaved like she did the other night because she was hurt—upset about *you*."

For an instant Max was dumbfounded. Then the colour rushed into his face. He gave a laugh.

"My *dear* little Iris. I've never heard such rubbish!"

But Iris, having gone so far, now went further.

"It's true, *it's true*, Max! Cindy has been in love with you ever since she came back from Cornwall."

"Ridiculous!"

"It isn't. You men are so blind and *stupid*!" exclaimed Iris, her face hot and pink with feeling. "She must have shown it a dozen times but you just haven't *seen*. I don't say she's ever actually told me so but she nearly gave herself away the other day. She *is* crazy about you. She didn't mind a bit when Derek announced his engagement. She doesn't mind anything much except that *you* are going away. She believed you didn't care a fig about her so she went sort of berserk the other night."

Another silence.

Max felt his heart beating so fast that he wondered if the whole wide world could hear it. This thing that Iris was telling him seemed to open a vista so dazzling that he hardly dared gaze upon it. It was as though she unloosed a floodgate—and a torrent of feeling rushed out and altered him for ever. Now he was incredibly, *a man in love.*

"I only wish you were right," he muttered, "and that Cindy did feel like that about me."

Iris drew a deep breath. So her instinct had been right; Max *did* love Lucinda. She said, bravely:

"Well, she does. Go and see her, Max. She's been so dreadfully miserable."

"Iris, if I really thought what you say is true——"

"Well, I am sure it is——" Iris said bravely.

"How fantastic!" said Max on a hushed note, then suddenly caught Iris up and whirled her round, kissed her firmly on both cheeks and set her down again.

"You're a darling—an absolute darling. I *will* go and tell Cindy how I feel and I swear I won't leave her house until I've made her repeat herself, what you've just said to me."

Lucinda was standing at the window of the sitting-room when Max's car rolled up and she saw him step out of it.

For her it had been a tiresome day so far; tiresome in the domestic sense. The 'daily' hadn't turned up. Mummy had a date with the dentist and had had to go out. Lucinda had been 'messing around' as she called it, with a mop and a duster. Daddy had gone out shopping at Harrods which he so often did on a Saturday morning, and Lucinda had nothing to look forward to but a visit from Max this afternoon which she knew was only in order to say goodbye. He was supposed to come between three and four. She had never felt more depressed. She had had a bad night. She had lain awake thinking about Max and a future which held little happiness for her, even though everybody said how lucky she was to be going to live in the South of France. She didn't even feel it was pleasant these days not to have to get up and queue for a bus in the rain every morning, and go to work, and come home feeling too tired to do anything much but have supper, look at T.V. for an hour then go to bed. Nothing pleased her.

She had received several letters from her godmother lately telling her how wonderful life was going to be with the de Malignys. Always with that accent on the 'nice boys' she was going to meet. Lucinda didn't want nice boys. She didn't want anybody but Max. And Max was leaving London the day after tomorrow, and in all probability she would never see him again. Worse still—he would take away with him a completely wrong impression of her. She wasn't really that gay, frivolous girl she had pretended to be. She wasn't.

She was shaking some dust out of the long satin curtains at the front window when she saw Max arrive. Why now—at half past twelve, she wondered crossly. She wouldn't have time to change, or do her hair, which was just hanging down her back, tied with a ribbon. And she had on slacks and an old jersey. Her nose was shiny and she looked *awful*.

She marched to the front door and opened it. It had been raining. There was also a strong wind blowing. A gust of wind blew into the hall and shivered through Lucinda. She exclaimed:

"Oh, goodness . . . shut that door quickly . . . there's a howling draught!"

"Sorry," he muttered.

She was overcome by the sight of him as usual, but she felt nothing but a desire to snap. She snapped at him now.

"I thought you were coming this afternoon? I'm not really ready for you."

"Sorry," he muttered again. "I'd better go away again."

"Oh, no, now you're here——" She opened the door wider.

He followed her into the sitting-room. The big thrilling moment had fallen so flat that it almost made him laugh. He even began to wonder if Iris had been talking a lot of damned nonsense. Rather angrily he took off his damp coat and threw it on a chair. Cindy picked it up.

"That's Mummy's best velvet upholstery—you'll get into trouble with her."

"I must say you're making me feel very welcome," he said resentfully.

She threw the coat out on the hall chair and came back, glowering at him through her lashes.

He saw that she had no make-up on and she looked very pale, with enormous angry eyes. Those slacks and the big fisherman's jersey and the long hair tied with a bow made her look like a kid of sixteen; like she had looked, he remembered, when she first went to see him at his hotel the night after that fatal engagement party. He had been filled with doubts about her then. Now, he had no doubts. He knew that he had misjudged her and that he had conducted himself like an unpardonable fool. Yet he felt suddenly a tremendous surge of thankfulness that he had not lived to see her married to Derek.

"You're off the day after tomorrow, aren't you?" asked Lucinda on a high note.

"Yes."

"I shall envy you the sun."

"H'm," he nodded.

"Have you seen Iris?" She was groping desperately for things to say. Outwardly she was angry; inwardly filled with misery, and a certain amount of self-pity because she truly believed that this was the end of her whole life's joy.

"Yes, I've just come from Iris," he said.

"How was she?"

"She showed me the letter from Dr. Brill-Burrie."

Lucinda flushed darkly.

"She needn't have. You can't be interested in it."

"Only in a vague way. But I've known for a long time that you were all he wrote about you."

She gave an unhappy laugh.

"Thanks very much."

"Look," said Max between his teeth, "we're getting no-where—fast."

Now she opened her eyes wide.

"Might I ask where we are *supposed* to be getting?"

"Oh, Cindy," he said in a voice of profound passionate feeling. "I love you, darling. I love you so very much."

If the walls of the house had fallen in and she had been suddenly caught up in the gale and blown into a void, she could not have been more surprised—or shocked. She felt herself vibrating from head to foot.

She stammered:

"I—I don't know what you're talking about. You must be mad."

"I am," said Max. "Madly in love with you. I've just told Iris so. I've known it for a long time but I've been too damned deaf, blind and dumb to admit it. But I can't go to

Kenya without telling you. I don't in fact intend to go back to Nairobi at all until you promise to marry me."

She cupped her burning face with both her hands and shook her head incredulously.

"Don't, *don't!*" she said. "You're just making this all up. You were horrified by me the other night. You walked out."

"I was a pompous fool. No—I was jealous—madly jealous," he corrected himself. "I knew that night that I was in love with you. I knew it on Christmas Eve too. But I still felt it my duty at that time to try and bring you and Derry together."

"Oh, Max!" whispered Lucinda, shaking her head again, as though it was too much for her. "We both seem to have been at cross-purposes."

Then she was in his arms, as she had been under the mistletoe in Iris's house—the long line of his body strong and demanding against her own. Their embrace was almost an anguish. Now neither of them misunderstood or pretended any more.

Lucinda's arms were around his neck. Her eyes closed, her lips warm, moving under his. He kissed her again and again; mouth, cheeks, hair and her long sweet throat. He kept murmuring her name:

"Cindy . . . Lucinda . . . my darling . . . *darling* Cindy! This is absolutely marvellous. *You're* marvellous. You're going to marry me, *me*, Cindy, and I'm going to postpone going back to Nairobi till I can take you with me."

She nodded, her cheeks wet with happy tears. She heard her own dazed voice.

"I love you madly, darling Max. I knew it when I was in Cornwall."

He was about to say: "*So Iris told me*," and then, foolish man though he was, remembered to be more tactful.

THE END

OTHER ROMANTIC NOVELS FROM THE
QUEEN OF ROMANCE

☐	01459 8	The Noble One	17½p
☐	12959 X	The Strange Meeting	20p
☐	12792 9	Climb To The Stars	20p
☐	14985 X	The Untrodden Snow	20p
☐	12359 1	Gypsy Lover	20p
☐	15124 2	House of The Seventh Cross	20p
☐	10882 7	Wait For Tomorrow	20p
☐	01065 7	I Should Have Known	20p
☐	14877 2	Love And Desire And Hate	20p
☐	15084 X	The Unlit Fire	20p
☐	15085 8	Brief Ecstasy	20p
☐	15097 1	You Have Chosen	20p
☐	15110 2	Shatter The Sky	20p
☐	15121 8	Those Who Love	20p
☐	15809 3	Swing Of Youth	20p
☐	16038 1	Arrow In The Heart	25p
☐	16082 9	All That Matters	25p
☐	16083 7	A Love Like Ours	25p
☐	16080 2	Put Back The Clock	25p
☐	15808 5	Strange Rapture	25p
☐	15810 7	The Wild Bird	25p

All these books are available at your bookshop or newsagent, or can be ordered direct from the publisher. Just tick the titles you want and fill in the form below.

....

CORONET BOOKS, Cash Sales Department, Kernick Industrial Estate, Penryn, Cornwall.

Please send cheque or postal order. No currency, and allow 5p per book (4p per book on orders of five copies and over) to cover the cost of postage and packing in U.K., 5p per copy overseas.

Name...

Address...

....